M. J. Rhodes

His Holiness Pope Pius IX and The Temporal Rights of The

Holy See

As Involving The Religious, Social, And Political Interests of The Whole

World

M. J. Rhodes

His Holiness Pope Pius IX and The Temporal Rights of The Holy See
As Involving The Religious, Social, And Political Interests of The Whole World

ISBN/EAN: 9783337064518

Printed in Europe, USA, Canada, Australia, Japan

Cover: Foto ©Raphael Reischuk / pixelio.de

More available books at **www.hansebooks.com**

HIS HOLINESS POPE PIUS IX.

AND THE

TEMPORAL RIGHTS OF THE HOLY SEE,

AS INVOLVING THE RELIGIOUS, SOCIAL, AND POLITICAL INTERESTS OF THE WHOLE WORLD:

(WITH A NOTICE OF SOME IMPORTANT PASSAGES IN THE HISTORY OF POPE PIUS THE SEVENTH;)

BEING

AN ADDRESS DELIVERED AT A MEETING OF THE CATHOLICS OF RICHMOND, YORKSHIRE, NOVEMBER 27, 1859,

BY M. J. RHODES, ESQ., M. A.

REVISED AND ENLARGED BY THE AUTHOR,
WITH APPENDIX.

WITH THE APPROBATION OF

THE LORD BISHOP OF BEVERLEY,

AND RESPECTFULLY DEDICATED, BY PERMISSION, TO HIS LORDSHIP.

LONDON:
THOMAS RICHARDSON AND SON, 147, STRAND;
9, CAPEL STREET, DUBLIN; AND DERBY.
MDCCCLIX.

TO M. J. RHODES, ESQUIRE,
RICHMOND, YORKSHIRE.

My dear Mr. Rhodes,

I thank you for allowing me to see your little work in defence of the Temporal Authority of our Holy Father the Pope, and you have my cordial approbation and blessing in proposing to publish it.

With kind regards,

I am, my dear Sir,

truly yours,

✠ JOHN,

BISHOP OF BEVERLEY.

York, Dec. 10th, 1859.

TO

THE RIGHT REVEREND THE LORD BISHOP

OF

BEVERLEY

(BY HIS LORDSHIP'S KIND PERMISSION)

THESE FEW PAGES ARE MOST RESPECTFULLY

DEDICATED

AS A SMALL TESTIMONY

OF

VENERATION AND RESPECT

FOR

HIS LORDSHIP'S PERSON

AND

SACRED EPISCOPAL OFFICE

BY

HIS VERY OBEDIENT HUMBLE SERVANT

THE AUTHOR.

Richmond, Yorkshire.
Feast of the Immaculate Conception,
1859.

" Disguise it how men will, there is one great central question which rises above all others, and concentrates, in love or in hatred, for defence or for attack, the enkindled hearts of the millions of civilised men. Amidst the rivalry of nations, the plots and counter-plots of statesmen, the musterings of armed forces, and the heated conflicts of public writers; this one question towers out predominant, and divides the world into two distinct and opposite arrays.

" Shall the Sovereign Pontiff, the representative of Christ, the veritable head of Christianity, be hurled from his temporal throne, or shall he retain that position of freedom and independence which he has held for more than a thousand years?"

Pastoral Letter of the Lord Bishop of Birmingham, Nov. 15th, 1859.

HIS HOLINESS PIUS IX.

AND

THE TEMPORAL RIGHTS OF THE HOLY SEE.

I.

When our adorable Lord and Saviour made His trium-
phal entry into Jerusalem, and the whole air rang with
the hosannas of the multitude, some of the Pharisees said
to Him, "Master, rebuke thy disciples;" and He replied,
"If these shall hold their peace the stones will cry out."

If I may with reverence adopt those words of my
divine Master, I would say, that on the occasion on which
we are met together, if we were to keep silence, the stones
would cry out. Yes, the very stones would reproach us!
The consideration of the position of our holy and venerable
Pontiff at this moment of trial is enough to cause emotion
in the most stony of hearts.

I say, moreover, that if we were silent on the subject
of the temporal interests of the Papacy at this time, the
stones of our old abbeys, whether in the sweet meadow,
by the meandering stream under the shady trees, or in
the midst of towns, where the houses cluster round them;
the stones of our old cathedrals which our Catholic ances-
tors built; and the stones of our parish churches, which
their piety also raised and endowed, and by the side of
which their bones repose, (God in His mercy rest their
souls!) all these stones would call out against us. I
say, too, that the stones of the halls where our children
play, and the hearth-stones round which they gather; yes,
and the buildings where our citizens meet together in
social and friendly intercourse; and the stones of old St.
Stephen's, or of that newer building which has taken its
place, where our parliament now meets to legislate for the
country's weal, they would reproach us too.

By this metaphor, I mean to assert that the temporal
rights of the Holy See are most intimately connected
with our dearest and our most sacred interests, *religious*,
social, and *political;* and that is the main point about
which I am about to speak, although I shall touch on
other subjects as they come in my way.

II.

Pope Pius IX.   Our first duty, however, is towards our most
holy Lord Pope Pius IX., who at present so
nobly fills the Chair of St. Peter. His position, at this
moment, is sublimely grand, and at the same time pro-
foundly touching. If there is a splendid spectacle on
earth, it is that of a man in elevated rank suffering for
truth and justice sake. If there is a touching spectacle
on earth it is that of a Father calling on the faithful ones
of his family to sympathize with him, and to pray with
him, in behalf of other children who have gone astray, who
have turned their backs on him, forsaken him, and despised
his authority. And both these spectacles we see in our
present beloved Holy Father.

That he suffers, and suffers deeply, we know by many
means. Just when the war was breaking out I read an
account of his giving audience to about 150 persons, a
great number of whom were French. It stated that
" after he had passed through the ranks, and blessed each
in particular with love and affection, the Holy Father
addressed them all, and said:—' My dear children in
Jesus Christ, I have just blessed each one of you, with all
the effusion of my soul; nevertheless, before leaving you,
my heart yearns to give you once more my benediction.
We are on the eve of very important events. God only
knows what He reserves for us all. You know that I am
the visible head of the Catholic Church; you are its members. We form the church militant, and if the Pope is
attacked, you know it is not against the individual it is
directed, but against Catholicity altogether, of which he
is the head and the chief. Gather close around me, unite
every day your prayers with mine, thus let us assail heaven
with a holy violence. Oh ! if you knew, my children, how
great is the strength of prayer; how great its power before
God ! Let us not cease, then, one instant, to pray for His
Church, for His spouse so beloved !' After these words,

pronounced with an emotion which found its echo in the heart of each one present, the Holy Father gave once more his benediction, which drew tears from nearly all who had the happiness to receive it."

I read again of him, full of that love which all good and noble men entertain for children; how, when some French family was presented to him, and there was a boy among the number, he asked that the boy should be left with him for the day. He took him round his palace, and pointing especially to that celebrated picture by Guido, representing St. Peter crucified with his head downwards, our Holy Father said to the boy, " There, my child, that is *my* picture." And that *is* his picture—his picture not only in suffering, but in courage and meekness, following in the steps of the holy Apostle, bearing his cross like him.

What is the purport of all his cries to us? What are they but the cries of a suffering father? How full of suffering are they! And what immense cause he has for suffering! Let us reflect for a moment upon his position. In the first place, his elevated station of course gives him many means of information which we do not possess. He knows well enough many dangers that the Church and the world have passed through, of which we know nothing, because he is in constant communication with the envoys of the Emperor of the French, and others. He knows too, many a cloud hanging over us now, of which we have no idea, and is uncertain whether it will break over us or not. He knows too the clouds on the distant horizon; and all this knowledge adds to his pain.

Again, how he feels the weight of his responsibility. Take the case of a man of this world, some sovereign or other person who has no fear of God in his heart, but who cares for his kingdom without caring for his people, who has a mere earthly end in view, one busied in making money, in getting a good name, or gaining dominion;—such a man has no cares of conscience. He has a conscience to prick him, I know, but he manages to smother that, and he goes on and looks out for those means which suit his purpose, caring not what God thinks of them if man is not offended, heeding no man's interests but his own, studying only self aggrandizement.

Not so with our Holy Father; he is the Vicar of Christ upon earth; he has the interests of his Master to look after; he has the interests of 200 million souls to care for, and we know that he would rather give up life itself than forfeit one tittle of those interests. You see, then, the weight of responsibility he has upon him.

His tiara may be decked outside with diamonds, but its weight is that of lead, and its internal lining is of the thorns of the crown of Christ.

Added to all we have this most horrible and wicked rebellion against the most loving and tender of Fathers.

Who that has ever been admitted to the presence of Pope Pius IX., who that has ever knelt under that fatherly hand, and heard his loving "God bless thee, my son,"* but must carry the remembrance of that moment through all future years; and, by memory's aid, see again and again that paternal countenance beaming with heaven's own light, calmly radiant with a benignity, a dignity, a cheerfulness which words cannot express, which nothing but the grace of God can give, which befits that Holy Pontiff, on whom God has conferred the honour beyond compare, of declaring to the nations that no shadow of a question remains concerning the fact of the divine revelation of the Immaculate Conception of her, whom all generations revere as blessed. Does not this entitle us to say of him as the inspired writer sings of Simon the high priest?

"In his days the wells of water flowed out, and they were filled as the sea above measure.

"He shone in his days as the morning star in the midst of a cloud, and as the moon at the full.

"And as the sun when it shineth, so did he shine in the temple of God.

"And as the rainbow giving light in the bright clouds, and as the flower of roses in the days of the spring, and as the lilies that are on the brink of the water, and as the sweet smelling frankincense in the time of summer.

"As an olive-tree budding forth, and a cypress-tree rearing itself on high, when he put on the robe of glory, and was clothed with the perfection of power."†

What that noble bearing and countenance expresses, is expressed too by his conduct at the present moment. Behold his conduct amidst his sufferings! What can

---

* Iddio ti benedica, figlio mio !
† Ecclesiasticus, chap. L.

exceed its grand nobility, its Christian meekness, its gentleness? No violence, no angry words, in the midst of his troubles; dignified but humble, courageous and fearless, but at the same time quiet, meek, resigned; so that, as has been said of his crucified Lord, when heaven and earth and hell beneath combined against him, there is one thing which cannot be, do your worst; you can never bring contempt upon that venerable head.

What Christian greatness in every appeal he puts forth, in every answer to dutiful sympathy! Ever asking prayers for himself under these heavy trials, he never fails to ask them for those poor misguided rebels also. " Pray," he says, " pray for my poor children who have left me; pray not for their destruction; pray for their conversion; pray for their salvation; pray that they may be brought back." It reminds us of the cry of holy David of old, " Oh, my son, Absalom; oh, Absalom, my son, my son!" Is it not like that? It comes from the fond yearning heart of a father who cannot bear to see his children suffer, even through their own fault, of a father who knows that the position in which God has placed him, compels him, as a matter of duty, to act with firmness towards those children if they persist in their wicked rebellion. For the patrimony of the Church which is committed to him, he has sworn at the foot of the altar to transmit intact to his successors. That property is not his own; it belongs to us all; it belongs to the whole Church, to the whole world we may say; it belongs to God, and he cannot forfeit any portion of it.

I say that those appeals of a Father to his children are touching beyond what words can express; there shines throughout them the Christian spirit of seeking peace and concord, wishing no ill to his enemies, but only desiring their conversion. Let me read you a short prayer which he lately ordered to be said throughout the Roman States:—

" God of peace, lover and guardian of charity, grant to all our enemies peace and true charity. Vouchsafe them remission of all their sins, and deliver us by Thy mighty power from their snares."

When the war arose, the Holy Father bad his children pray,—the world obeyed, and the waves of war were hushed; but, alas, in their stead rebellion reigned triumphant, and reigns so still.

Ah! methinks I hear you say, all this is true, but why this indulgence of feeling?—why dwell so long on this? Well! I own it, but what shall I answer? Forgive, I beg you, forgive a filial heart which, knowing its father comes of kingly race, knowing that he is nobler than earth's proudest great ones; pardon such a heart if, grieved and torn by the daily insults which a thoughtless time-serving press heaps on that venerated Father's head, it seeks a momentary solace in culling the sweetest words, the sweetest thoughts at man's command, to lay at that dear Father's feet, and so strives to offer what little reparation it is able; pardon it for lingering on in the contemplation of his sorrows; and, oh I am sure of it, heartily do we all wish we could send across the seas, and across the mountains, an expression of the feelings which actuate us towards our dear Holy Father.

"O Holy Father," we would say, "accept our heartfelt homage, our filial sympathy; accept our sorrow that any of your children should be found heedless of their duty to such a Father; accept our firm resolve, by God's grace, to do all that in us lies to make amends to you for their unfilial conduct, and to win them back to you. Bless us, and pray for us, that we may be strong in this resolution. Bless us, and pray for us, that we may be worthy children of so great, so high-minded, so noble a Pontiff."

And we may conceive he would answer the respectful filial sentiments of sympathy and affection which we so desire to express, in some such words as these:—

"Yes," he would reply to us, "Yes, my dear children, with all my heart I bless you; but while I accept with joy this testimony of your affection, I wish you to be thoroughly convinced of the justice of my cause. Examine, I beg of you, deeper and deeper the sacred rights which I am defending; they are not so much mine as God's; they concern you as much as they concern myself."

III.

No party question.   They concern us, they concern our country, they concern the whole world. I speak not as a partizan. I have not a particle of party spirit in what I say; I am a Catholic, heart and soul; I am so from the innermost convictions of my being; because, from the bottom of my heart I believe, and am ready, by God's assistance, to die for my belief; that the Catholic Church, alone, is built upon " the foundation of the apostles and prophets, Jesus Christ Himself being the chief corner stone ;" because I believe that to her alone, Christ has committed the custody and guardianship of the religion which He founded upon this earth; that He Himself lives in her and animates her whole system; that she is the one, and the only one, commissioned to bear His name and preach His truth before the nations; and that in no other name but His, which she alone can bear; and in no other faith but His, which she alone can teach; is there salvation to be found. But, precisely, because I am heartily a Catholic, therefore I am no partizan; because you can conceive no two opposites in the world so great, as the Catholic spirit and a party spirit.

Party spirit is always seeking its own interests, seeking the advancement of some human opinion, seeking the interests of a *party;* in short, it is true to its name. And in like manner the word Catholic denotes what it is, *universal.* The Catholic Church is animated by that divine and universal love which breathes in the breast of God Himself; it is animated by the very Spirit of God. That Spirit which fills the world was poured out upon her on the day of Pentecost, and the very centre and sum of her system is love to all the world. And if she warns those who are treading in the path of error, following the broad road of destruction, is that want of charity? It is the fulness of her charity which leads her to use those words of loving strength to warn men of their danger. Will a mother use soft words to a child on the brink of a precipice? Will she let it dally with the danger?

But, let a man's religion be what it may, be he Turk, Infidel, or Pagan, be he Protestant or be he Catholic; and be his position in this world what it may, be he clothed in rags, or adorned with the purple of kings, the Catholic Church has a heart to love him; she will seek his best interests as none other will. In each individual man she sees a being made after God's own image, she knows he has an immortal soul, meant for a throne in heaven, if he do but use God's gifts aright, and turn not from the light and grace God offers; she sees there a soul for which Christ died; and she knows that soul is of a value unspeakably higher than all the kingdoms of the world. So she can never be other than the truest friend of all mankind, and her interests are the real interests of the whole human race.

Therefore do I raise my voice in behalf of the temporal rights of the Papacy. Those rights are, humanly speaking, *necessary* for the Church to fulfil the work of love with which God has intrusted her for the benefit of all mankind; all mankind are interested in defending them, and all true friends of mankind will unite in maintaining them.

IV.

Pope Pius VII. and England.   To shew you the large heart which beats in a Papal breast, I will bring forward an instance, which, if it be a lengthy one, at the same time contains a history of which Englishmen cannot be too often reminded.

Englishmen, I fear, or rather, I hope, (for if their memories were not in fault we might expect greater respect for the Holy See) have forgotten what Pope Pius VII. underwent at the hands of the first Napoleon, because he unflinchingly refused to set aside his character of Pope; in other words, of the common Father of mankind; and close his ports against British ships. Let me tell you what passed. I commence with an extract from a letter written by Napoleon I. to Pope Pius VII., and dated February 13, 1806.*

"Most holy Father, I have received the letter of your Holiness of the 29th of January. I enter into all your troubles. I quite understand that you must have difficulties: you can avoid them all by walking in a straight path, by not entering into a labyrinth of politics, and yielding to considerations for those powers, who, in a religious point of view, are heretics and out of the Church; and who, in a political point of view, are at a distance from your States, incapable of protecting you, and who can only do you harm. *All Italy shall be subject to my law.* I will not touch the independence of the Holy See in anything. I will even pay the expenses occasioned to it by the movements of my army. But the condition must be, that your holiness shall have for me in temporal

---

* These letters are given at full length by Monsr. le Chevalier Artaud, Histoire du Pape Pie VII.

matters, the same regard that I have for you in spiritual, and that you cease from useless consideration (*ménagemens*) towards the heretical enemies of the Church, and those powers who can do it no good. *Your Holiness is Sovereign of Rome, but 1 am its Emperor.* All my enemies must be yours. It is not fit, then, that any agent of the King of Sardinia, any Englishman, Russian, or Swede, should reside at Rome, or in your States, nor that any ship belonging to these powers should enter your ports."

What did the Holy Father reply? He wrote direct to Napoleon on the 21st of March, the letter is before me, and I give you the following extracts.

"We commence," thus writes the Pope, "with that which your majesty demands from us: you wish that we should drive from our States all Russians, English, Swedes, and agents of the King of Sardinia, and close our ports to the ships of the three above-named nations; you wish us to abandon our state of peace, and enter upon an open state of war and hostility with these powers. Will your majesty permit us to answer in the plainest terms, (*avec une netteté précise*) that, not on account of our temporal interests, but because of the essential duties inseparable from our character, we find it impossible to accede to this demand.........We, the Vicar of that Eternal Word, ' who is not the God of dissension, but the God of concord, who came into the world to drive away enmities, and to preach peace to those who are afar off, as well as to those who are near,' (such are the expressions of the apostle), how can we deviate from the instructions of our divine Founder? how contradict the mission to which we have been destined?

" It is not our will, it is the will of God, whose place we occupy on earth, which prescribes to us the duty of peace towards all, *without distinction of Catholics or heretics, of neighbourhood or distance, of those from whom we expect good, or those from whom we expect evil.* It is not permitted us to betray the office committed to us by the Almighty, and we should betray it, if, from the motives adduced by your majesty, that is to say, if, as regards heretical powers, which can only do us harm, (it is thus your majesty speaks), we were to accede to demands which would lead us to take part against them in war."

Now let us see how Popes can act as well as speak. The

2

Protestant historian, Alison,* tells us that after this intrepid answer from Pius VII., the troops of Napoleon spread over the whole Papal territory and surrounded Rome.

"The French minister soon after intimated, that, if the Pope continued on any terms with the enemies of France, the Emperor would be under the necessity of detaching the Duchy of Urbino, the March of Ancona, and the sea-coast of Civita Vecchia, from the ecclesiastical territories; but that he would greatly prefer remaining on amicable terms with his Holiness; and with that view he proposed, as the basis of a definitive arrangement between the two governments: '1. That the ports of his Holiness should be closed to the British flag, on all occasions when England was at war with France. 2. That the Papal fortresses should be occupied by the French troops, on all occasions when a foreign land force is debarked on *or menaces* the coasts of Italy.' To these proposals, which amounted to a complete surrender of the shadow even of independence, the Pope returned a respectful but firm refusal, which concluded with these words: 'His majesty may, whenever he pleases, execute his menaces, and take from us whatever we possess. We are resigned to everything, and shall never be so rash as to attempt resistance. Should he desire it, we shall instantly retire to a convent, or the Catacombs of Rome, like the first successors of St. Peter; but think not, as long as we are entrusted with the responsibility of power, to make us by menaces violate its duties.'

"The overwhelming interest of the campaign of Jena and Eylau, for a time suspended the attention of Napoleon from the affairs of Italy, but no sooner was he relieved by the peace of Tilsit from the weight of the Russian war, than he renewed his attempts to break down the resistance of the ecclesiastical government, and was peculiarly indignant at some hints which he had heard, that the Pope, if driven to extremities, might possibly launch against his head the thunders of the Vatican. A fresh negotiation was nevertheless opened; Napoleon insisting that the Court of Rome should rigidly enforce the Berlin and Milan decrees in its dominions, *shut the ports against the English flag,* permit and maintain a permanent French

---

* Hist. of Europe, ch. lvii.

garrison at Ancona, and allow the march of French columns through their territories.

"The Pope expressed his readiness to accede to these propositions, and submit to their immediate execution, *except the actual declaration of war against England.*"

I am sure the generous hearts of Englishmen, whether Protestant or Catholic, or whatever their religion, would respond to this great fact, if they did but know it. It is much to be lamented that, at this day, Englishmen do not inform themselves better concerning the real facts of any case which comes before them; they too often gather their information from distorted reports in newspapers, without examining authentic sources.

The next step was this. The Emperor insisted on these conditions, *and the declaration of war against England.* A large body of French troops entered Rome. On the day of their arrival, the Pope called in the French ambassador, and said to him:—"The Emperor insists on everything or nothing: you know to what articles proposed I will consent; *I cannot subscribe the others.* There shall be no military resistance: I will retire into the Castle of St. Angelo: not a shot shall be fired, but the Emperor will find it necessary to break its gates. I will place myself at the entry; the troops will require to pass over my body; and the universe will know that he has trampled underfoot him whom the Almighty has anointed. God will do the rest."

"Insults and injuries," Alison proceeds, "continued to be heaped upon the head of the devoted Pontiff."......
"He continued, under these multiplied injuries, to evince the same patience and resignation; firmly protesting, both to Napoleon, and the other European powers, against these usurpations, but making no attempt to resist them."
......" The head of the faithful was no longer anything but a prisoner in his own palace; but all Napoleon's efforts to overcome his constancy were unavailing."......" The last act of violence at length arrived. On the 17th of May, a decree was issued from the French camp at Schœnbrunn, which declared 'that the States of the Pope are united to the French empire; the city of Rome, so interesting from its recollections, and the first seat of Christianity, is declared an imperial and free city;' and that these changes should take effect on the 1st of June following. On the 10th of June, these decrees were announced

by the discharge of artillery from the Castle of St. Angelo, and the hoisting of the tricoloured flag on its walls instead of the venerable Pontifical Standard. "Consummatum est !" exclaimed Cardinal Pacca, and the Pope at the same instant; and immediately, having obtained a copy of the decree, which the dethroned Pontiff read with calmness, he authorized the publication of a bull of excommunication against Napoleon, and all concerned in that spoliation, which, in anticipation of such an event, had been sometime before prepared by the secret council of the Vatican. Early on the following morning, this bull was affixed on all the usual places, particularly on the churches of St. Peter's, Santa Maria Maggiore, and St. John, with such secrecy as to be without the knowledge or suspicion of the police. It was torn down as soon as discovered, and taken to General Miollis, who forthwith forwarded it to the Emperor at his camp at Vienna. The Pope expressed great anxiety, that care should be taken to conceal the persons engaged in printing and affixing on the churches this bull, as certain death awaited them if they were discovered by the French authorities; but he had no fears whatever for himself. On the contrary, *he not only signed it with his name, but had transcribed the whole document, which was of great length, with his own hand, lest any other person should be involved, by the hand writing, in the vengeance of the French Emperor."*

Is not this like the good shepherd who gives his life for the sheep? and are these the men who deserve to be despised and ridiculed as in the present English press, which teems with the grossest insults against the Papacy; insults which I am sure must offend the moral sense of every generous minded Englishman, be his opinions what they may?

But to proceed. Alison says that Napoleon, with apparent truth, has protested that he was not privy to the sacrilegious seizure of the Pope's person, which followed this noble conduct; but he adds, that his acts showed his approval of what had been done.

The French authorities agreed that it was necessary to obtain possession of the Pope's person. His palace was stormed, and at last, to prevent further violence, the doors were thrown open, and the French general, Radet, "in a respectful manner, pale and trembling with emotion, announced to his Holiness that he was charged with a painful duty, but that he was obliged to declare to him, that he must renounce the temporal sovereignty of Rome and the Ecclesiastical States, and that, if he refused, he must conduct him to General Miollis, who would assign him his ulterior place of destination. The Pope, without agitation, replied, that if the obligations of a soldier required of him such a duty, those of a pontiff imposed on him others still more sacred; that the Emperor might "cut him in pieces, but would never extract from him such a resignation, which he neither could, nor ought, nor would subscribe." Radet then ordered him to prepare for immediate departure, intimating that Cardinal Pacca might accompany him on the journey. The Pontiff immediately complied; and the French General having assured him that nothing in his palace should be violated, he said, with a smile, "He who makes light of his own life, is not likely to be disquieted for the loss of his effects." Their preparations having been quickly made, the Pontiff took his place in the carriage, with Cardinal Pacca by his side, and, escorted by a powerful body of French cavalry, soon passed the Porta del Popolo, and emerged into the open and desert Campagna. "Cardinal," said the Pope, "we did well to publish the bull of excommunication on the 10th, or how could it have been done now?" At the first post-house he wished to give some charity to a poor person, but, upon inquiry of Cardinal Pacca, he found that between them they had only a papetto, or tenpence. He showed it, smilingly, to Radet, saying, "Behold, General, all that we possess of our principality!"

This noble cheerfulness of a good and courageous conscience, is the very type and picture of the apostolic character, "sorrowful, yet always rejoicing; needy, yet enriching many; having nothing, and possessing all things."*

The same Protestant historian, from whom I have so largely quoted, adds remarks which are too striking to be omitted. These sad events took place in the year 1809. Alison observes that, in the year 1807, Napoleon had said in a confidential letter to Eugene Beauharnois,

" ' What does the Pope mean by the threat of excommunicating me? Does he think the world has gone back a

---

* 2 Corinthians, vi. 10.

thousand years? Does he suppose the arms will fall from the hands of my soldiers?' Within two years," says Alison, "after these remarkable words were written, the Pope did excommunicate him, in return for the confiscation of his whole dominions; and in less than four years more, *the arms did fall from the hands of his soldiers.*" He then refers to the account given by Segur: "The weapons of the soldiers," says Segur, in describing the Russian retreat, "appeared of an insupportable weight to their stiffened arms. During their frequent falls, they *fell from their hands;* and destitute of the power of raising them from the ground, they were left in the snow. They did not throw them away, *famine and cold tore them from their grasp.* The fingers of many were frozen on the muskets which they yet carried, and their hands deprived of the circulation necessary to sustain the weight."

He also quotes Salques:—"The soldiers could no longer hold their weapons; *they fell from the hands even of the bravest and most robust. The muskets dropped from the frozen arms of them who bore them.*"

Alison then proceeds:—" the hosts, apparently invincible, which he had collected, were dispersed and ruined by the blasts of winter; he extorted from the Supreme Pontiff at Fontainbleau, in 1813, by the terrors and exhaustion of a long captivity, a renunciation of the rights of the Church over the Roman States;* and within a year after, he himself was compelled, at *Fontainbleau,* to sign the abdication of all his dominions: he consigned Cardinal Pacca, and several other prelates, the courageous counsellors of the bull of excommunication, to a dreary imprisonment of four years amidst the snows of the Alps; and he himself was shortly after doomed to a painful exile of six on the rock of St. Helena! There is something in these marvellous coincidences beyond the operations of chance, and which even a Protestant historian feels himself bound to mark for the observation of future ages. The world had not gone back a thousand years, but that

---

* It must be remembered that no one more 'bitterly bewailed this act of human weakness than the high-minded Pope himself; he wrote privately to Napoleon to recall it, a week after it had occurred, and when he had obtained the assistance of his Cardinals, he formally revoked it three months afterwards. See an interesting article on Le Concordat de Fontainebleau, in the Correspondant for October, 1857.

Being existed, with whom a thousand years are as one day, and one day as a thousand years."

I rest my excuse for this long digression on the extreme importance and interest of these facts. Well might a great politician exclaim, when urged to declare war against the Pope, "First shew me, from history, any hand which has ever been raised against that power, and prospered!"

V.

As regards the present miserable rebellion in the States of the Church, I shall say but little in detail, because I am rather striving to explain and defend the principle which it violates, than to expose all its individual enormities.

The present rebellion in the Papal States.

But I cannot let it pass quite without notice; and I must observe, in the first place, that any one, who will attentively read the accounts which we receive from Italy, may see there is no proof whatever, that, the mass of the people in the Papal States desire any other government than the one which they possess. I am sure the Pope himself would not deny that reforms in that government may be required and desirable; and I am sure also that he would be the first to promote them if he could with prudence do so; he is prevented from doing so by the conduct of the revolutionary party; because (to use an English expression) when he gives an inch they take an ell.

When he came to the throne he gave ample reforms; and what did they do? They murdered his prime minister, and the Pope had to fly from Rome himself. The fact is, that the rebellious and infidel faction who agitate Italy, will be satisfied with no reforms; they want to be rid of the Pope altogether; and if they can accomplish this (which God avert) then they will want to be rid of all other authority, kingly and the rest, which stands in the way of their own lawless will. For the Italian people themselves, I have the greatest regard, only I wish they had more moral courage; I have lived long among them and I know their kind hearts; but I believe they are a timid people, and I believe they are really afraid of the dagger of the assassin, and that the fear of it prevents them from rising in defence of the Holy Father.

It is asserted that the Papal States are a hot-bed and a nursery for revolution throughout Europe, owing to faults in their government, which are assumed without any sufficient ground, and are alleged to be the cause of the existence of those secret societies whose net-work spreads like a foul disease underneath the whole of the seemingly fair outside of modern Europe. Now I firmly believe that the real reason why the efforts of these societies are so strongly directed against the temporal rights of the Papacy, is simply because that temporal sovereignty is the strongest and the firmest barrier in existence against anarchy and confusion. I believe it is this, and nothing less than this, which draws upon it the unquenchable hatred of those wicked spirits; and, I say, that to encourage their revolt against the temporal sovereignty of the Holy See, is to undermine the firmest thrones in Europe, and to expose her most flourishing states to the danger of democratical tyranny. Granting that some reforms might be of service, is rebellion to be recognized as the proper means for obtaining them? I do not deny but that there may be such an extreme case in which a sovereign may so utterly neglect his duties, be so tyrannous, so violate private rights and all natural law, that his subjects may be absolved from their allegiance. There may be such a case; but who will dare to say, who has ever adduced anything approaching to an assertion, that such is the case in the States of the Holy Father? The two strongest accusations of this kind which are brought against him, are really nothing, if a man will but look at them with the eyes of common sense.

One is the Perugia matter. What was that? A city urged on by foreign emissaries—for it is known that arms had been sent there, long before, from Tuscany—rose against its rightful rulers. Now, supposing Manchester, or some other large city in England, were to rise against the Queen, what would she do? She would send troops to put the rebellion down; and we should all think her perfectly right. Take the case of India. We know that we have just put down a bloody revolt in India, and we know that there are many accusations of cruelty brought against our authorities there. Now, be those accusations true or false, no one thinks of charging our beloved Queen with them; no one says it is the fault even of her prime minister. And if there were excesses committed *by individuals* among the Roman troops, (which I do not for a moment admit there were, but which, of course, in every such affair is liable to happen, nay almost impossible to prevent) why is the Pope to be made responsible for them? It is the old story of the complaints against the Christians in the days of persecution. An early Christian writer says that if the Tiber rose and flooded Rome, the cry was "The Christians to the lions! It is their doing." Or if the Nile did not rise and overflow its banks, it was still, "The Christians to the lions!" So in our own times, whatever happens in Italy, it is all "the Pope," it is all "priestly domination." The fact is, these men hate the Pope, they want to dethrone the Pope, nay more, they want to dethrone Christ Himself, and these are simply pretexts, and lame excuses.

Then, there is the Mortara case: I must say a word about that also, because it is so much misunderstood. I say again, if only looked at from a common-sense point of view, what can be simpler to any Christian mind? There is a law in the Roman States that the Jews are not to engage Christian servants; it is meant to prevent many evils, and is no doubt a wise and good law. This law was violated by a Jew who took a Christian for his servant. The Jew's child was at the point of death, and the servant baptized him. The child recovered, and grew to boyhood, and when it was found by the authorities that he was a Christian, it was thought fit to remove him from his parents, lest his Christianity should be (if I may use the word,) suffocated by Jewish influences. We all know that baptism confers spiritual life, Protestants as well as Catholics profess it; at least the Anglican prayer-book speaks of baptism as a new birth. Now, if our government suspected a father of administering slow poison to his child, to take away its *natural* life—if they had good reason to believe that the child's life was in danger, would they not feel it their bounden duty to remove that child from the parent's influence? And are we Christian men not bound to do the same to preserve *spiritual* life? That child's spiritual life was in danger; his heirship to heaven was in danger; Christ was in danger of losing a soul for whom He had shed all His precious blood. Was all that to be set at nought? I say it was a positive duty, not only of the Pope, it would have been the duty of any Christian government to have acted in the same way. The *Times* brought the case forward to show that there should be no Papal government, but a lay government, in

which such things would not occur; but how could it
escape notice that such an act would be as much the duty
of a layman as of a priest? What was done to the boy?
He was taken to school, is being carefully educated,
allowed to see his parents, is as happy as possible, and
rejoicing in being a Christian. I think, therefore, that
no reasonable, no Christian man, can lay any stress upon
that case.

It would be beside my purpose to enter upon a political
account of the Roman States; I wish, however, that persons would take pains to inform themselves before they
find fault; to touch only on one point, they would at once
perceive what a striking and favourable contrast the
Roman government presents over the Sardinian, in financial matters; and, as to a parliamentary system, what is it
worth, if, as in Piedmont, it is suspended the moment war
breaks out? In reference to the demand for the secularization of the Roman government, 1 shall have a word to
say further on.

VI.

¹ All Catholics, of
all nations, are
bound to defend the
Temporal Rights of
the Church.

Let me first, however, set before you the
ground upon which I maintain it to be the
general duty of all Catholics, whatever their
country may be, I might say of all men, if
they did but know it, to protect the rights of the Holy
See. Suppose it to be said, 'I acknowledge the *spiritual*
authority of the Holy Father, but why am I, an Englishman, to come forward in a political way, and use all my
exertions to protect the *temporal* rights of a foreign
prince?' My answer at once is plain. The Pope is not a
foreign prince to any Christian, to any human being.

Let me take an instance. I will suppose what
is probably an impossibility, but it will explain my
meaning. Let us suppose that the King of Portugal
became a priest, and was made Pope, still retaining
his personal rights to the kingdom of Portugal. Now,
suppose those rights to the crown of Portugal were in
danger, would all Catholics be bound to rise to do
their utmost to help him to support them? Certainly
the fact of his being Pope would tie us closer to him, but,
setting this aside, there would be no call whatever upon
us to assist him; the kingdom of Portugal might go, and
there would be no great loss to him, or to us; it would

be a mere personal loss, and he would have less care on his head, as those who wish to overthrow the Pope say of his present temporal Sovereignty. But the Pope's title to the temporal Sovereignty of the States of the Church, although it is in one sense independent of his spiritual power; that is, though he might lose the temporal, but could never lose the spiritual supremacy; still it is the natural consequence of his spiritual power, and is given him to ensure his full and free exercise of it.*

It is not a personal right. We do not, in defending him, defend King Mastai Feretti, but we defend Pope Pius IX. The States of the Church, as the name denotes, were given by pious men to God and the Church; they were given for the purpose of benefiting the sacred cause of religion, benefiting the Church; therefore, every member of the Church is not only interested, but is bound to do his uttermost to defend them. The Pope holds them in trust for us all.

Let me give you another instance. Suppose some malicious person strove by an unjust law-suit to get possession of the private property of the Mayor of this town, should we be bound to defend his rights? As his very good friends we should no doubt do our best in a neighbourly way, but we should have no especial call beyond that. But, if any property which he held as Mayor, if any rights

---

* In confirmation of this and many similar remarks which follow, I beg to refer to the authorities quoted in the Appendix; among them will be found an English translation of the Allocution delivered by our present Holy Father on the 20th of June last. I here subjoin an important extract from it, in the original Latin.

" Quamobrem cum Nos Apostolici Nostri muneris officio, solemnique juramento adstricti debeamus religionis incolumitati summa vigilantia prospicere, ac jura et possessiones Romanæ Ecclesiæ omnino integras inviolatasque tueri, et *hujus Sanctæ Sedis libertatem, quæ cum universæ Ecclesiæ utilitate est plane conjuncta,* asserere et vindicare, *ac proinde ipsius Principatum defendere, quo ad liberam rei sacræ in toto terrarum orbe procurationem exercendam Divina Providentia Romanos Pontifices donavit,* illumque integrum et inviolatum Nostris Successoribus transmittere, idcirco non possumus non vehementer damnare, detestari impios nefariosque perduellium subditorum ausus, conatus, illisque fortiter obsistere."

At the end of Section XII. will be found the open declaration of his Holiness, as to the *necessity* of the civil principality for the Holy See.

of the mayoralty were attacked, every townsman would feel bound to do what he could to defend them. It is precisely the same thing with the Pope, though of course his rights are more sacred. He is, as I said before, King *because he is Pope ; and because he is the Head of the Church, and holds these states for the good of the Church, therefore every member of the Church is bound to assist him in his duty of protecting them.* Let no one, then, say that it is un-English, or that we are going out of our way to help a foreign power. *He is not a foreign power in that sense of the word.* We know, that as a matter of fact, the Pope may be chosen from any nation under the sun.

And how important are those temporal rights ! Who can overrate their vast importance ? Ah ! we do not think enough of this. People do not sufficiently consider what would be the consequence if those rights were gone, and the Pope reduced to be the mere subject of some temporal Prince.

In the first place, can any of us be dutiful children of our God and Saviour, and consent to see the Head of His Church so reduced ? Is not the mere idea of the Vicar of Christ, the representative of God Himself, being subject to a temporal power, revolting to the law implanted in every human heart ?

VII.

Glance at the History of the Papacy.

If we take a glance at the history of the Popes, we shall see plainly how God has made temporal sovereignty a necessary accompaniment (I use the word, necessary, not in its absolute, but its ordinary sense) of their spiritual sovereignty, so that it grows out of it, and belongs to it, as its natural right. In the early ages of the Church, God was pleased to give a manifest testimony of her Divine origin, by miraculously supporting her and extending her limits without any human power, and in spite of superhuman obstacles. Her very existence and, much more, her growth under such circumstances was a miracle ; it ceased with her infancy ; when she reached maturity God supplied her with the temporal sovereignty, which, though no part of her essence, is nevertheless her natural and proper mode of action, and, as such, her right. If need were, God would again, most certainly stretch out His arm in miraculous defence of the Church and her Supreme Pontiffs; but, to uphold her without having recourse to human means, would be a departure from the ordinary laws of His Providence.

Let us go back eighteen hundred years; or further still,—to those days of old, when Daniel the Prophet explained the vision to the king of Babylon; how the stone cut out of the mountain, without hands, struck the great statue, and how the stone grew, and became a great mountain, and filled the whole earth; and that stone represented a kingdom which the God of heaven would set up, and which should never be destroyed, but should stand for ever.* There is the origin of the Papacy, for the Papacy is the centre, the concentrated life, the head and heart of that kingdom.

Thence let us pass on to the time when our Lord began His public life; when Andrew findeth his brother Simon, and brought him to Jesus, and Jesus, looking upon him, said:—"Thou art Simon, the son of Jona: thou shalt be called Cephas, which is interpreted, Peter," or in English, rock. And again, when in Cæsarea Philippi, that high promise was given,—"I say to thee, thou art Peter, and on this rock, (this Peter,) I will build my church, and the gates of hell shall not prevail against it." And later still, let us recall the threefold commission given to St. Peter by that eternal Word, whose words shall never pass away, "Feed my lambs; Feed my lambs; Feed my sheep."

This charge conveyed at the same time a right to the means required for its fulfilment, in such a shape as God's wisdom might provide.

Strong in the might of that divine commission the Galilean fisherman, mighty in his weakness and rich in his poverty, goes to plant his throne in proud and haughty Rome on her seven hills, the Babylon of the nations. And he enters her lordly streets, and gazes, with a sigh, on her luxurious palaces, which hardly covered the licentiousness that reigned within them; on her heathen temples, where vice was worshipped under the most beauteous idol forms; on her amphitheatres, reeking with human blood, where gladiators fought with beasts or with each other;

---

* Daniel, ch. ii.

where young senators and patricians assembled, decked in purple robes; and ladies in soft tissue clapped their delicate hands, and raised their tender voices with delight, when by a dexterous stroke some human heart poured forth its life-blood, and the gladiator fell quivering to the ground. That shout

> " He heard it, but he heeded not—his eyes
> Were with his heart, and that was far away;
> He recked not of the life he lost nor prize,
> But where his rude hut by the Danube lay,
> There were his young barbarians all at play,
> There was their Dacian mother—he their sire
> Butchered to make a Roman holiday :
> All this rushed with his blood."

The wickedness then reigning in Rome no tongue can paint, and this kingdom of the powers of darkness, that despised stranger now treading her streets was to overcome; that proud city was he to reduce to the dominion of the cross, to make it the centre of the kingdom of Christ. There was to be his throne.

What were to be the weapons by which he was to win it? Suffering and death. When he and his fellow-labourer, St. Paul, whether in the palace of Pudens, in their own hired house, or in the Mamertine prison, had ended their apostolic work of preaching and of baptizing, of planting the glorious kingdom of Christ, which silently but strongly grew under their hands with superhuman speed; then at last God took them to their reward; St. Peter was crucified with his head downwards, and St. Paul won the palm of martyrdom by the sword; bequeathing to Rome, in the words of an early writer, their faith with their blood.

O glorious apostles ! pray for us at this moment ! Pray for our Holy Father, your successor; may I not, without presumption, say, a successor worthy of your great name ?

What followed then? Three centuries of martyrdom, three centuries of suffering, three centuries of toil and hardships, of weary but brave endurance. Strengthened and marvellously consoled by the grace of God, the blessed martyrs shed their blood; holy Pontiff, valiant soldier, tender woman, infant child, gladly yielded their sweet lives for that dear Lord, who, on the cross, had redeemed them by His own. It was that blood which watered the roots of the Papacy, it was "that red rain which made the harvest grow;" it was that suffering which like winter's frost, and winter's storms, passed over the ground till the seed had taken firm root. Those were the rivets which fastened the Church to the rock of Peter. Pontiff after Pontiff died by the sword and by persecution; till at last, in the early part of the fourth century; after Constantine had ascended the throne; St. Sylvester, who had retired for safety to Mount Soracte in the neighbourhood of Rome, beheld armed troops on all sides approaching the place of his retirement, and turning to his companions with cheerful countenance he exclaimed, "Behold, now is the acceptable time: behold, now is the day of salvation." Then he went forth with joy to the soldiers, anticipating the martyr's crown. They led him to the Emperor, but not to martyrdom.

For Constantine, warned in a vision, had sent for the holy Pope to beg at his hands the sacrament of baptism, and the story goes, that when those healing waters cleansed his soul, his body was likewise cleansed of a foul leprosy with which he had been afflicted. In a short time St. Sylvester was seated in the imperial Lateran palace.

Then rose splendid churches and gorgeous basilicas too numerous to relate, and where once the devil had been worshipped under the name of the false god Apollo, there was founded, over the tomb of the Prince of the Apostles, that venerable former church which bore his name, and is now replaced by the present St. Peter's. Nor were rich endowments wanting, and God sent sunshine on His Church, though its gleams were fitful, and many a fierce blast was yet to come. Still those three centuries of suffering had been enough to root well and firmly the goodly tree which was now to rear its lofty head, and give shelter to the birds of the air.

From those three centuries, as well as from many subsequent events, we may learn how the Catacombs become the Church's home, when she is shorn of that temporal sovereignty which is the natural right of her supreme Pontiffs.

Now mark the wondrous ways of Divine Providence. Constantine builds him a palace of pleasure, and founds a noble city far away from Rome, on the sunny shores of the Bosphorus, and there he removes the seat of empire.

Never, after the time of which I speak, did an Emperor reside at Rome; there was, indeed, an Emperor of the West, but Rome was no more his capital. St. Peter was now to be its King. Emperors did not, indeed, cease occasionally to persecute the Church; even so late as the seventh century we find a holy Pontiff, St. Martin, borne ignominiously from Rome to Constantinople to the presence of the Emperor Constans; we see him laden with chains, shamefully abused, and sent to die in exile in the Chersonese, because, in the heroic fulfilment of his sacred duties, he had dared to condemn a heresy respecting the person of his Divine Lord; concerning which the Emperor, like men now-a-days, thought there had been enough disputing, so in his wisdom of this world he had forbidden either side to utter another word.

If Popes were now in subjection is not this just the treatment God's truth might expect from the spirit which breathes all round us? proclaiming, as it does, aloud, the sacred rights and liberties which belong to falsehood! bidding men forbear to claim that truth can be but one; and deeming it unchristian to teach, that it is sinful to question truths which God has Himself revealed?

Before we quite turn from these centuries of suffering let me ask, "Is there any heart so callous as to wish to send the Popes back to such times?" We have seen the result of their having no temporal power. The only means they had of defending the independence of their ministry, says a French writer, was to die; and they died like heroes and like Christians. But do we wish it to come over again? Let no man say that it cannot come over again in these days. Witness the horrors of the great French Revolution; the massacre of the Carmes! Witness the reign of terror in Rome, when the Pope was absent! Witness but lately Count Anviti falling under the daggers of savages. Let travellers write to the *Times* and express their astonishment at finding Garibaldi the most gentlemanly of heroes, instead of the ruffian they expected; let fair speeches and fine words abound as they may; trust it not! it is "seeming! seeming!" a fair silken mask which hides a hideous monster's face beneath it! That boasted moderation need not surprise us while the rebel's work is prosperous; they can afford to be moderate while unopposed; God grant their present quiet be not the tiger's pause before his spring; be not the lull before a storm of blood ready to burst upon that fair Italian land.

VIII.

And now we approach a most important topic—the rise of the temporal power of the Popes. There is this which plainly marks it Historical origin of the Pope's Temporal Sovereignty. as the gradual silent work of God. No one can point, with precision and certainty, to the precise time when it did arise. This much, however, is plain; the Popes never sought it, they never grasped at it, they took no means to obtain it. God put it in their hands, and, before God, they are bound to keep it. It grew as the tree grows from the soil. You cannot say when the acorn first bursts its shell and the lordly oak springs forth. Tell me whence the broad river draws its waters;—tell me of all the streams, all the little rivulets and fountains that feed it, and then I will tell you every source which gave rise to the temporal sovereignty of the Popes. Like everything natural, everything providential, we can only catch indications of it here and there, in the days of its infancy, for I speak of times long before Charlemagne.

There have been several theories about it. Some have said that it was given by Pepin, and Charlemagne, and Louis le Debonnaire. Doubtless these sovereigns used their efforts in behalf of the temporal rights of the Holy See, and augmented those rights, but they did not found or confer upon it the original temporal sovereignty. Others have said that the temporal power of the Popes arose when the Greek Emperors retired; but that cannot be, because, before that time, we find signs of its existence.*

As I have said, it grew imperceptibly, as all God's works grow. No doubt the retirement of the Greek Emperors from Italy, very much assisted to promote it; and no doubt Charlemagne and Pepin helped to protect it, but it is one thing to protect a sovereignty which already exists, and another to bestow that sovereignty. If we consider those stormy times, we shall not wonder at our being unable to ascertain the precise moment when it

---

* An early number of the *Civiltà Cattolica*, observes that even from the times of St. Gelasius and St. Symmacus, (the 5th century), "we find many acts of civil jurisdiction exercised in Rome by the Supreme Pontiffs, as manifestly appears from Anastasius, the librarian."

3

commenced, and to trace its early growth ; nor shall we wonder that the times themselves produced it, as their natural produce.

It was a fearful thing that breaking up of the old heathen Babylon, when the whole world was convulsed with the death pangs of the giant Roman empire, and the foolish Romans still hugged their old idolatry, for they were still half pagan,—when the Goths, and Huns, and Vandals, and other endless barbarian hordes poured out their wild multitudes upon Italy ;—when Alaric came in his fierceness, in spite of the hermit on the Alps, who fell on his knees and implored him to stop and not desolate the kingdom,—but he replied, "I hear the voice of God within me, saying, go and lay waste Rome." For the idolatry of Rome was to be chastised, but St. Peter and St. Paul did not forget their flock. The same mysterious impulse which had sent forth Alaric to desolate Rome, inspired him to command that the churches of St. Peter and St. Paul should be respected, and that every one who entered those churches should be spared. He entered the city with his barbarian army and gave it up to pillage. One of his captains, entering the house of a nun, asked her for treasures ; by a wondrous inspiration, the holy woman led him straight to a room, and flinging open the door, displayed to his astonished gaze, the rich treasures and the sacred vessels of St. Peter's ; the accumulated wealth of the gifts of the pious. She said to him, "I have these treasures in my keeping, but they belong to St. Peter ; I cannot restrain your arm—touch them if you dare." The soldier, departing in amazement, informed Alaric, who immediately ordered that those treasures should be held sacred and conveyed at once to the Church of St. Peter, and, that every one who accompanied them, should be protected. Then, in the midst of the wild barbarian sacking of the city, might be seen a procession of Christians bearing aloft the sacred vessels, raising high their voices in hymns and songs, unhurt, uninjured, bearing their treasures in safety to the church, assisted by the very hands of the pillagers of the city.

What a spectacle was that! There was the hand of God stretched forth in visible protection of the rights of Peter. No wonder men sought St. Peter's shadow, and took refuge under the protection of his mighty but peaceful sway.

The Romans still persevered in their wicked idolatry in spite of the chastisements they had received, and then came Attila the Hun, with his 500,000 followers, who are described as more like demons than men. And still St. Peter, in the person of his successor the holy Leo, interposed in defence of the people; Attila, while yet in the North of Italy, was met by that intrepid Pontiff; not at the head of an army, but with a few ecclesiastics; in the calm, quiet, majestic dignity of our present holy Father. What passed we know not, but this we know, the course of that human flood was turned. It is said that Attila afterwards declared that he had seen St. Peter and St. Paul in the air, threatening him if he advanced.

Well might the Romans hail as King a holy Pope, who, by his single voice, animated by the might of God, saved them from the merciless fury of that barbarian chief and his 500,000 savages. But all was not over yet. Man's wickedness was not over, nor had God ceased to scourge. Genseric came, one of the Vandals. He set sail from Africa, and when asked by the pilot, "Where shall I steer?" He answered, "Leave that to the winds; they will take me to the country God is angry with." He landed near Rome. Again the holy Pope went forth with a few unarmed ecclesiastics, and though he did not succeed in turning him back, he obtained for his people the best terms he could, and proved himself the Father of his flock.* The horrors of that time were so great that when the Greek General, Narses, took the city in 552, it was the fifteenth time it had been taken by an army within sixteen years.

St. Gregory the Great, who lived at the end of that century, exclaims, at the conclusion of his Homilies on the prophet Ezechiel, "Blame me not if henceforth I cease from these discourses; on all sides are we surrounded by the sword; on all sides in imminent danger of death. Some return to us deprived of their hands, others we hear of in captivity, others slain. I am compelled to restrain my tongue from the exposition of Scripture, for my soul is aweary of my life. My harp is turned to mourning, and my organ into the voice of those that weep." The same holy Pontiff used his exertions to redeem the cap-

---

* I must thank that excellent popular work, the Clifton Tracts, for the assistance it has rendered me.

tives, and even permitted and commended the sale of the sacred vessels of churches to raise sums for the purpose.

Ah! people soon find out who is their true Father! their true Protector! What throne can boast a grander and a firmer title than grew up naturally for the Popes under these circumstances? When the Greek emperors abandoned Italy altogether, after long using their power in it for their mere selfish ends, the Popes alone could rule the land. The Church was the only regularly organized society at the time, and the Pope was the only person at the head of any organized body. All the rest was confusion, and it naturally followed that those who wished for peace and order wished him for their sovereign.

IX.

Charlemagne did not confer the Temporal Sovereignty. A few remarks are called for upon the claim sometimes raised, on the ground that the Popes received their temporal sovereignty from Charlemagne. It has been said Charlemagne gave it, and that, therefore, his successors can take it away again. Now, in any case this would be strange reasoning, that if I give a thing to God, or even to man, my descendants may take it away again when they please.

But Charlemagne did not give it. He did not claim any sovereignty over Rome; otherwise we should not find him, as in the year 774, when he visited that city, asking and obtaining permission from the Pope to enter it, that he might pay his devotion at the Churches.[*]

It is a fact, however, that the Pope, when a part of his dominions were invaded and torn from him by the Lombards, after vain efforts to recover them by peaceful means, applied to Pepin, the father of Charlemagne, to rescue them from the hands of the invader: Pepin did so, and restored them to the Pope.

But in his act of donation, there is not a word respecting the city of Rome, nor concerning other territory dependent upon that Duchy; he treats it as indubitably already subject to the dominion of the Pontiff. Charlemagne confirmed the donation of Pepin, and added other

---

[*] Rohrbacher, Hist. de l'Eglise, liv. liii., who refers to Anast. in Adr.

territory. His son Louis, styles both his father and grand-father *restorers* to the Holy See, of the rights which it already possessed.*

As regards Charlemagne, I cannot do better than give you another extract from the same letter of Pope Pius VII. to Napoleon I., from which I have already quoted on another point. That venerable pontiff wrote thus :—

" Your Majesty says that our relations towards you are the same as those of our predecessors towards Charle-magne. *Charlemagne found Rome in the hands of the Popes;* he recognized, he unreservedly confirmed them in the possession of their domains, he augmented them with new donations, he never pretended to any right of domain, or superiority over the temporal sovereignty of the pontiffs, he never claimed from them either dependance or the homage of a subject.....

" But, in fact, ten centuries since the times of Charle-magne have rendered useless all further investigation. An undisturbed possession of a thousand years is a title the most clear which can exist between sovereigns; the fact of that possession has proved, that, whatever may have been the understanding (*les intelligences*) between Charle-magne and the Pontiffs, in those obscure times and under those tempestuous circumstances, the Holy See has never, in reference to her temporal domains, entertained any other relations with the successors of Charlemagne, than those which exist between every absolute and independent sovereign, and other sovereigns."

X.

The Popes did what they could for Europe in anointing Charlemagne as Emperor, but what times came after Charlemagne! The world was like a huge unruly boy, and played with human life and human rights as a reckless child plays with butterflies. Those were times of heroic goodness and diabolical vice. It was an iron age; and who was it that tamed that proud age, schooled the world in that its boyhood? Who but the Popes?

Those Popes are accused of arrogance. I wish that the persons who accuse them of it would consider the times

The Popes and Modern Europe.

---

* Civiltà Cattolica, Nov. 1850.

they lived in.   Popes had to deal with such men as
our King John; who, once when in want of money, as
those kings always were, asked from a rich Jew at Bristol
the sum of 10,000 marks.   The Jew was not disposed to
give it.   Accordingly, he was sent to prison, and by the
king's orders one of his teeth was to be drawn every
morning till he gave the sum required.   There was no
chloroform in those days; and, if there had been, not
much chance of his getting any.   They began with his
back teeth, and for seven days he bore the operation,
but when the eighth morning came his courage failed,
and he gave security for the 10,000 marks.*

Those were the wills that the Popes had to break; those
were the tyrants they had to deal with, and was that to
be done by fair words and soft silken measures?   The
devil then stalked without a mask; he did not put on
the honied tones of diplomacy, and dress like a fine
gentleman, as he does now-a-days, concealing the foulest
wickedness under the sacred names of liberty, patriotism,
and the like.

What a noble spectacle those high-minded Popes present, battling to the death for right against lawless might!
Men such as St. Gregory VII., who, after a life-long
struggle in the cause of God, was forced to fly from Rome,
and breathe his last on the shores of Salerno.   Oh! how
those dying words of his shine all down the page of history, grander than the grandest conquests it records:—
"I have loved justice and hated iniquity; therefore I die
in exile."

Noble, sainted Pontiff, pray for your successor now!

'Twere long to tell all the benefits rendered to humanity
by the Church in those wild times, and the Popes were the
life and the strength of her sacred cause.   Protestant his-
torians have acknowledged how much civilization owes to
her; and the battle so often fought by her heroes in behalf
of the poor and the oppressed, in behalf of liberty and of
God, fought against tyrant kings, who neither feared God
nor regarded man, that battle of suffering could never
have been sustained but for the irresistible might of the
appeal to Rome.   What would have become of our own
St. Anselm or St. Thomas à Becket without the Popes
to support them?   Their great names have been defamed,

---

* Lingard.

and their noble histories falsified by the flatterers of Kings, whose wickedness they dared to resist when duty plainly demanded resistance; but, as might be expected, in these later days, when men are awakening from the slumber of prejudice; it is becoming evident to all that these very men, whose cause was the cause of the Popes, and with whose names have been coupled every offensive epithet, who have been styled proud, arrogant, and ambitious, were in reality humble and heroic servants of their God; the truest friends to their country; the protectors of the oppressed; friends to the friendless, and fathers to the poor.

Take alone that marvellous victory achieved by the Church over those mail-clad barons, when she succeeded in obtaining a cessation from war and bloodshed for four days in the week, besides the seasons of Advent, Lent, and all solemn festivals! What an insight this Truce of God, as it was called, gives us into the state of those times and into the services the Popes rendered to the world, for, as I have said, the Popes were the mainstay of every such achievement.

It was the Popes, too, who befriended and encouraged learning and the fine arts; they taught the world its alphabet: till at last the silly upstart world began to give itself airs; it learned Latin and Greek; it took, in short, a literary turn, and began to fancy it knew more about things than the Popes themselves, who had schooled and educated it from infancy.

Then came what Wordsworth, in his stanzas on St. Bees, designates as,—" Reformation's sweeping overthrow;" when men were taught that doctrines revealed by God were to be subjected to their own private criticism; that the voice of the Holy Ghost no longer spoke visibly on earth, but that each man must seek it in himself, as his own fancy might lead him. Principles which I hesitate not to say, if carried to their result, are utterly subversive of all religion and of all society. Happily the men who hold them very seldom act upon them, they mostly follow some party of fellow-men with whom they agree, or some leader they choose (perhaps unconsciously) for themselves. Of course, having no longer God for their leader, they are but troops of blind led by the blind; but still, inconsistent as it is, more order is thereby kept than if each blind man was to grope about for himself, and dispute the road with every neighbour he met.

Against these new woven wiles of Satan the Popes did
what they could ; but, alas ! too many of their children
gave no heed to them, and there was nothing for it but to
pray, and hope for better things.

Then were opened to the Church the distant regions of
the East, as well as Africa and America, and she sent
forth her sons, warriors of Christ, to win for Him those
heathen souls.   But it was a dreary worldly time for the
states of Europe.   Although there are saints who shine as
stars all through it, still it was a seed time of infidelity and
irreligion ; one Catholic King* was even found, who, for
his own wretched ends, could befriend the Ottomans in
their attack on the dominions of a brother Catholic.
The Popes had done their utmost to resist the withering
grasp of the Mussulman ; and had Christendom but been
true to them and to herself, it may be many a fair region
of Asia, and those holy plains of Palestine, might now
be flourishing under Christian rulers.

Popes cannot command impossibilities, though they
have done wonders ; it is my object to show you that they
are the true fathers of mankind, and that all through they
have done their best for the truest interests of their children.

During these last ages of civilization who can say
what the world has lost by turning a deaf ear to its
Father's voice ?   If war is not so frequent, is it not far
more bloody ? and is it not so frequent as to disgrace the
civilization we boast of ? Do congresses, where selfish interests contend, and where diplomatists endeavour to balance
nicely the power of each, as if each were ready to grasp for
himself if he dare ; are these assemblies, where expediency,
too often, well nigh rules all things, to be compared to the
voice of the Father of the Faithful, entrusted by God with
the common interests of all, and lovingly and impartially
arbitrating among them ?   But it is useless to dwell on
happiness so imaginary, except that the consideration of
what Europe is, and of what it might have been, had civilization attained its growth under a Father's fostering,
guiding hand, may well deepen our reverence for that
authority of which men make so light.   Although the arts
and sciences come not directly within the sphere of that
authority, yet, had its warning voice been duly heard, we

---

* Louis XIV.

should not have witnessed those high gifts of God prostituted to the service of man's vilest passions; we should have escaped that outcry of shallow learning which declared that science was opposed to revelation, and we should sooner have attained the knowledge which profounder research has now afforded, that the deeper you penetrate into the secrets of science, the more plainly does she show herself the handmaid of religion; the more strongly does she confirm (alas! that men should need it!) the voice of God. Better, by far, would it have been for scientific research itself, if, like dutiful children, her sons had listened to the Church and to the Popes, protesting that any deduction contrary to divine revelation was by that very fact proved false.

But, alas! the world became impatient of the yoke of Christ, it ran wild in its wilfulness, and now nothing will content it but to endeavour to reduce to the state of a subject the Vicar of Christ himself.

Let it not be said that it was merely in the days of old, such as we have glanced at, that the Popes required the protection afforded them by their temporal sovereignty; or that in these days their ruling influence is less needed. How would the Church have fared without it, in the hands of such men as Louis XIV., Joseph II. of Austria, Napoleon I., or the present Victor Emmanuel of Sardinia, the Archbishop of whose capital is even now in exile for conscience sake, and whose government has laid sacrilegious hands on possessions consecrated to the Most High? and without the independence afforded by their temporal sovereignty to the Popes, how could they have adequately protected the Church in all these cases? That sovereignty both obtains them greater respect in the eyes of mankind at large, and also ensures them that freedom of action so necessary to the due exercise of their high pastoral duties. It is, so to speak, a palace which shelters them from the storms of the world, and from whence they may, in calm safety, watch over the welfare of mankind.

Behold that long line of Popes! behold that venerable time-honoured dynasty of those Fathers of the world! what earthly dynasty of kings or emperors can compare with it? And shall we sit by and see this most sacred, most beneficent of powers shorn of its temporal dignity; dishonoured in the eyes of men, because robbed of its earthly sove-

reignty; crippled in its work of love because deprived of
the means with which God Himself has endowed it freely
to labour for the benefit of the universe ?

Forbid it every sense of veneration for what is most
high and most sacred on earth ! Forbid it every consideration of prudence in behalf of the common interests
of the whole human race !

XI.

Proposed secu-
larization of Ro-
man Government.
But at least, it is said, consent to the secularization of the Roman Government. In
other words, let the Pope cease to be Pope
in his own dominions. If anything is meant by the
secularization of the Roman Government, it is either
to place it in the hands of a lay ruler, or in other words
to deprive the Pope of his temporal sovereignty ; or it
means that he is merely to reign as a constitutional
monarch, after the pattern of England, laymen being
entrusted with the reins of government under the Pope.
It cannot mean merely the admission of laymen to the
numerous though more or less subordinate offices of government, for that is already very largely done ; and moreover, it must be observed, that the ecclesiastical state is
not a caste, it is supplied from the ranks both of the pea-
sant and the prince, it is open, after due training, to all
whom it pleases God to call to that high dignity,—it would
therefore be a manifest hardship on the people, to *exclude*
the clergy from even the lower offices of state, by opening
them *only* to the laity ; at present they are open to both,
and neither class can justly complain.

A moment's reflection will show, that it would be
manifestly inconsistent with the Pope's office to make
over the reins of government to laymen, or to subject himself to the trammels of a constitutional government. We
know very well that in a constitutional monarchy like the
English, the power rests in reality with the Houses of Parliament ; it is true the Sovereign's consent is required to
their Acts, but it is rarely, if ever, withheld. Suppose for
a moment this were the case in Rome, and suppose the
parliament there, was to pass a divorce bill ; such as has
lately, alas ! become the law in England ; appointing a
court where man sits to put asunder those whom God has
united, those who have sworn before God that death alone

shall part them ! suppose such an act to pass in a Roman parliament, the Pope must suffer martyrdom itself rather than consent to such a violation of God's law.

Again, short of this, how many measures in reference to education, to the property of convents, to matters more or less connected with religion, might not a lay-government desire to enforce in opposition to the Pope, their Sovereign ? It is plain such a state of things would be anomalous, it would at once place everything in a wrong position ; no thoughtful man, it seems to me, could seriously advocate it, unless an enemy of the Papal power altogether.

The same reasoning which proves the necessity of the independence of the Popes, and consequently of their temporal sovereignty, proves also the necessity of their remaining perfectly free from the influence of their own subjects. They are in a position different from that of any other sovereign, they are the representatives of God upon earth, and, as such, they must be absolute and perfectly free rulers in their own domains, assisted by those councillors their wisdom may select. They have responsibilities before God which none other has, they are entitled therefore to a freedom of action before man on grounds which no other sovereign can allege.

XII.

Having considered the subject in a general point of view, I now invite your particular attention to my assertion that the temporal rights of the Papacy are most closely connected with the *religious, social,* and *political* interests of all mankind.

That their most important *religious* interests are concerned is so evident, that it is surprising any one should require to be reminded of it. True indeed it is, that wherever the Pope may be, and whatever may be his temporal condition ; be he reigning in Rome, or prisoner at Fontainebleau, breathe he his blessing on the world from the balcony of St. Peter's, or from the recesses of the catacombs; spiritual Father of the world, true Pope he must ever remain.

In this sense his spiritual authority is altogether independent of the temporal. The temporal may be destroyed utterly, but the spiritual cannot be lessened in itself any more than you can injure the soul by maiming the body; but, by that or other means, you may impair the soul's full power of external action, and though the spiritual power of the Popes can never *entirely* lose its external means of action, (for that would be tantamount to its destruction,) still its freedom of action might be so impaired as to deprive us of the *full* benefit we should otherwise derive from its blessed influences, and which, indeed, is vouchsafed to us at present. The world cannot pluck the sun from the heavens, but it can obscure it by its mists; it can never overthrow the Papacy, but it might succeed in interposing its vile fogs and murky clouds between our longing eyes and that sun of God's Church below! We might still see our way, but could no longer bask in the full warmth of those cheering beams.

The temporal Sovereignty of the Popes is the human and natural means appointed by Providence for a divine and supernatural end. God, of course, might have chosen other means, but it is a fact that He has chosen this. He might dispense with human means altogether, but man must never abandon them, excepting at God's command. It is God's way to work through certain means; to expect Him to change His way, and to work by a constant miracle, is presumptuously to tempt Him; it is to throw oneself from a pinnacle of the temple as Satan wished our Lord to do, because God had promised that His angels should take charge of Him.

Now, viewed in this light, reflect how important, and, in a human sense, necessary, the temporal independence of the Holy See is, both to the actual free exercise of the supreme Pastoral office, and to our own participation in the fulness of those blessings of which God has made His chief Pastor the channel.

It is necessary that the Pope should be a perfectly free agent, and it is necessary that all the world should know him to be so. If he is not so he cannot adequately fulfil his duties; and if he is not known to be so the world will not be sufficiently assured that it is really Peter who speaks in him. One of the conditions essential to render the Pope's voice authoritative in matters of faith and morals, is, that he should speak not as a mere individual, but as Pope. Now, perfect freedom of action is universally recognized as a condition that is necessary to enable the Pope to speak to the universal Church, effectually and beneficially, as Pope; and the temporal sovereignty being the divinely appointed means both for securing this freedom of action in itself, and for assuring the Catholic world of its existence, we are, on this account alone, most deeply concerned in upholding it.

But this is not all; besides faith and morals, besides that range of questions appertaining to faith and morals, in which we believe the Church possesses the divine promise of never failing protection from error; there are the administrative rights and duties of her chief Pastor. It is the concern of the whole Church, and the concern of each one of her children, that the Sovereign Pontiff should exercise these powers with all possible freedom of action. The more unrestrained their exercise is, the wider will be the influence of our holy Religion, the fuller our participation in the benefits of St. Peter's heaven-commissioned rule. But who can calculate the evils which might ensue, even in these matters, from the Head of the Church being subjected to the control of any temporal power? Witness the unhappy concessions wrested by Napoleon I., at Fontainebleau, from his captive, Pius VII., but no sooner wrested by the Emperor, than revoked by that noble-hearted Pontiff.

Consider the multiplicity of subjects nearly affecting the interests of the Church, which come before the Supreme Pontiff and the different courts or congregations over which he presides. Excellent as the members of those congregations may be, can we reasonably expect every one of them to be a hero in virtue, and proof against all the influences which might be brought to bear upon him by a secular government, desirous to influence his voice? Even suppose every one of these numerous individuals to be a very angel of fortitude and constancy, it is manifest that prudence itself might often, under such circumstances, require the abandonment of some design from which the Church at large, or that of a particular province, would have reaped incalculable benefit.

Take the case of the establishment of the English Hierarchy. Let any one reflect upon the blessings it has brought with it,—our peaceful synods, the restoration of diocesan action, and the promise of many more benefits to come. But what an outcry on the part of the English Government against it at the first! and what frenzy seized on the English people, or a large portion of them! Not all, for I well remember, myself, a Protestant friend at the time, who was unutterably shocked by the foul insults against things most sacred which that time brought forth, so that he exclaimed, " Can this be a Christian nation ?" He said to himself—" Well, after all, it was not thought necessary to ask the Emperor's leave before St. Titus and St. Timothy were ordained Bishops of Crete and of Ephesus."

He thought the language of our Cardinal Archbishop truly great and worthy, and he was not alone in his disgust at the madness which carried away our countrymen. I remember perfectly well another excellent Protestant friend remarking to me, " Can it be that the reason for proclaiming the establishment of the Hierarchy so near the 5th of November, was the anticipation, on the part of those friendly to it, that it would cause such an amount of angry folly in the country as to shock all thoughtful people, and win them to their side ?" So true is it, that, to whatever amount of outward opposition any bold act in a good cause may give rise, there will be many a secret heart who will appreciate your act aright unknown to yourself ; you tremble at the momentary tempest you have aroused, but the day of judgment will satisfy you of the lasting good which has really been wrought.

But I am digressing ;—my object is to show how certain we may feel that the English Government would have moved heaven and earth to prevent the establishment of the Hierarchy, had there been a secular government in Rome, through which they could have influenced the Holy Father ; and, possibly, in that case, considerations of prudence might have compelled him to abandon that most beneficial measure. How many cases may suggest themselves of this sort ! Say, some favourite education scheme of the government, which the Church apprehends it would be dangerous or impolitic to agree to. The secular government at Rome might be interested in being on good terms with the rulers of the country where the pernicious scheme is being hatched ; they are glad to do them a service, and they throw every obstacle they can in the way of the Pope and his advisers, to prevent them from coming to a decision adverse to the government they are themselves interested in serving. I need not cite other instances, the danger seems to me self-evident.

Truly those must entertain an exalted idea of Ecclesiastical authorities, who imagine that they would always be proof against such efforts to pervert them from the paths of justice, in the numerous matters which come before them concerning the temporary government and affairs of the Church, and not involving any decision on points of faith and morals.   No one can esteem and reverence them more highly than myself, but I know they are human, and we are not justified in allowing them to be placed in a position, which would expose them to superhuman temptations in their high and arduous task of the administration of the affairs of the Church for the common benefit of us all.   Nor must we allow them to be placed in circumstances which might compel them from sound reasons of prudence, to abandon any measure which is in itself desirable.

Statesmen of this world have not changed their nature. It is not so long since the late Emperor Alexander of Russia remarked, at Erfurth:—"I experience no difficulty in affairs of religion; I am the head of my own Church." *
We know that in the present day, as in the days of our forefathers, the secular power is always endeavouring to encroach on the ecclesiastical, to interfere as regards marriage, and a multitude of other matters within the Church's province; now, as of old, we require the strength and protection afforded by an appeal to Rome, and what would become of us if that central power was itself suffering oppression from the state, and consequently unable to afford us all the assistance we require?   Why should it be unlikely to happen that the Pope, if a subject, might be banished or imprisoned in consequence of the firm performance of his sacred duties, as so often happens in the case of other bishops?   He might be separated from his Cardinals, or be more or less deprived of necessary means of information, a thousand impediments might be put in his way.   True he could never cease to be Pope, but his action or speech might be trammelled; true, whatever his condition, all faithful hearts must ever render him a homage no Emperor could command; but he might be reduced to such a state of external degradation that many a lukewarm soul might fall away, and his high office be exposed to the danger of contempt in the eyes of the multitude.

If God brings it on us, He will certainly provide for all

---

* Alison.

this; but woe be to us and to our children, if we bring it on ourselves by apathy or indifference!

I cannot do better than quote, on this subject, the following noble words of the present Bishop of Orleans, in his recent protest. That venerable prelate speaks as follows:—

"You talk of the respect due to the wishes of peoples. Well! we Catholics, we too are a people; we are two hundred millions scattered over the face of the earth; and it concerns our dearest and our most sacred interests that the temporal sovereignty of the Pope, which is intimately connected with the dignity, with the independence, and with the free action of the Church, should not suffer any detriment. We will not permit, and the general conscience of Catholics cannot permit, at least without an energetic protest, (which will be heard by God, because it is the protest of right and of weakness, against violence and oppression.) No! we will not permit the Papacy to be attacked or morally cast down from its throne by the infamous force of fraudulent compulsion.

"You say that you can lay your hands on the Sovereign without doing injury to the Pontiff. Beyond all doubt the temporal power is not of Divine institution; who is there that knows not this?—but it is of Providential institution, and who so blind as not to see it? True, for full three centuries the Popes had no other independence but that of martyrdom, but most certainly even then, they were entitled to another manner of independence: and Providence, who visibly supported them, but who does not always use miracles as its means, established the liberty and the independence which is necessary to the Church, on a basis more legitimate than any sovereignty in Europe. History proves it beyond a doubt; all great men have acknowledged it, and true politicians know it well. *This is the work of centuries*, said Napoleon I. with his accustomed quickness of perception, *this is the work of centuries, and the centuries have done well.*"

. "Yes, it is necessary, for the Church's liberty and for our own, that the Pope should be *free* and *independent*. It is necessary that this independence should be *sovereign;* it is necessary that the Pope should be *free, and that every one should see him to be free;* it is necessary that the Pope should be free in his own States, as well as free from all external influence. This is necessary for the quiet of the Church and the tranquillity of our consciences; this is requisite, so that, in the wars too common among Christian powers, he may securely maintain that neutrality which belongs to the common Father of all the faithful. Nor is it sufficient that the Pope should be free in the internal court of his own conscience; it is requisite that his liberty should be apparent; that in the eyes of all he should be manifestly free; that he should be known to be so; that all should believe it, and that no one should be able to raise even a doubt or a suspicion concerning it. Even if in the bottom of his soul he were free, should he externally appear to be, I will not say oppressed, but merely subject to the power of a foreign prince; for example, of the Emperor of Austria, or of Russia, we should all suffer from it; he would not seem to us sufficiently free, and a natural distrust would perhaps lessen in many, it may be unconsciously to themselves, the respect and obedience which they still would owe to him. In fact, it is necessary that his action, his will, his decrees, his word, and his sacred person, should enjoy the full and free exercise of authority, rising above all influences, all interests, all human passions; so that neither discontented interests, nor irritated passions, should have even the shadow of a right to raise complaints against him."......

"This doctrine is confirmed by the example of Pius IX. himself, when on occasion of his flight from Rome, to which he was constrained by the outrages and violence of rebels, he made this solemn protest:—"Among the motives which have induced us to this separation, the most important is, that we may possess full liberty in the exercise of the supreme power of the Holy See; which exercise, under present circumstances, might be suspected by the catholic universe to be no longer free in our hands."

I have already once cited the first Consul,—now hear what he said, when he aspired to the glory of Charlemagne: "The institution which maintains the unity of the faith, that is the Pope, guardian of Catholic unity, is an admirable institution....The Pope is far from Paris, and it is well: he is neither at Madrid nor Vienna; and precisely on this account we support the yoke of his spiritual authority. The same must be said at Madrid and at Vienna. Can it be supposed that if the Pope were at Paris, the Viennese or the Spaniards would consent to receive his decisions? Happy is it for us that he inhabits

4

that ancient Rome.....It is the centuries which have done this, and they have done well. For the government of souls, it is the best, the most beneficent institution which can be conceived. I maintain these assertions, not from the obstinacy of a devotee, but from the conviction of reason."*

But I may appeal to higher testimony still. Our present Holy Father himself, in his recent Encyclical Letter to the Catholic Hierarchy throughout the world,† in a very marked manner says:—

"WE PUBLICLY DECLARE THAT THE CIVIL PRINCI-PALITY IS NECESSARY TO THIS HOLY SEE, IN ORDER, THAT, WITHOUT ANY IMPEDIMENT, IT MAY BE ABLE TO EXERCISE ITS SACRED POWER FOR THE BENEFIT OF RELIGION."

Such words, at such a time, and from such lips, will surely prove sufficient to rouse all our hearts!

XIII.

Social interests involved. I need but refer to the pages of history, throughout, to convince any impartial mind of the debt *Society* owes to the Papacy. When all else was chaos; the Papacy and the Church, by precept, by exam-ple, and by hard enduring struggle with the iron will of tyrants and oppressors, succeeded in establishing and in nursing the elements of order and of liberty, in modern Europe. It was the Popes whose voice was ever raised

---

* Thier's Hist. du Consulat et de l'Empire.

† An English translation of this letter will be found at full length in the Appendix, but I here subjoin the original Latin of the passage which I have quoted, with its immediate context.

"Dum Nos rebellionis hujusmodi actus et reprobamus, et dolemus, quibus quædam tantum populi pars turbatis in iisdem provinciis injuste adeo respondet paternis studiis, curisque Nostris, ac dum *necessarium esse palam edicimus Sanctæ huic Sedi civilem principatum, ut in bonum religionis sacram potestatem sine ullo impedimento exercere possit,* quem quidem civilem Principatum extorquere eidem comnituntur vaferrimi hostes Ecclesiæ Christi, Vobis in tanto rerum turbine præsentes damus litteras, Venerabiles Fratres, ut aliquod dolori Nostro solatium quæramus."

alike in defence of the just title of kings to the obedience
of their subjects, and of the just title of subjects to protection and fatherly care, in place of oppression, from the hands
of sovereigns.

It was the Popes who maintained the holiness of the
family tie, and whose constancy never quailed even
beneath the angry frown of kings, in upholding to the
uttermost, the inviolable sanctity of marriage. When
Philip Augustus of France sought to be freed from his
wife Ingelburga of Denmark, and obtained that in open
court, in her presence but herself unheard, the marriage
should be declared void; then the cry of that injured
woman arose to Rome. She understood not the language,
but as well as she could, she exclaimed on hearing the
sentence of the French court, "Ill done France! ill done
France!"—and she added, "Rome! Rome!" "Sublime word," adds the French historian, "of innocence
oppressed, appealing to the protector God had given her in
the Chair of St. Peter." And Rome did her justice, though
the contest with that proud king was a hard one; he sub-
mitted at last, but not before in his rage he had exclaimed,
"I will turn infidel; happy Saladin who had no Pope!"

Where, but in the history of the Popes, will you find
such instances as this, of determined, unyielding defence
of injured female innocence? of a persevering contest, not
for temporal power or possession, but simply for the
enforcement of a moral and religious duty from the strong
towards the weak?

The sacredness of marriage lies at the root of all social
order, and it cannot escape our notice how it is precisely
in those countries which have turned away from the voice
of the Popes that the marriage bond has become loosened,
so that even divorce courts are established to legalize
adultery, and the law of the land acknowledges as permis-
sible, that which the command of God condemns.

But, although, alas! so many heed no more the voice of
Peter, it still exists for Catholics; it exists moreover as a
solemn protest before God and man. Therefore, beware
how you weaken that voice or obscure it, by allowing it to
be robbed of the means which Providence has given for
its full and free exercise.

There is another and a most important manner in
which the present, or any, attack on the temporal rights
of the Holy See, becomes an attack on the social interests

of mankind. Both the foundation and the keystone of social order are contained in the divine principle and command.—" Let every soul be subject to higher powers : for there is no power but from God : and those that are, are ordained of God. Therefore, he that resisteth the power, resisteth the ordinance of God."*

Never was there a grosser violation of this principle, or breach of this command, than in the case of the present revolt in the Romagna and the Legations. What pretext have those rebels save their own lawless will? What is it but the cry,—"We will not have Christ's Vicar to reign over us, give us a king like other nations, or let us rule ourselves?" And think you the strong flood of human will, when once it bursts this moral barrier, will stop till it has overflowed the world? On what plea can you repress discontented murmuring in any country, if you once yield to this pernicious violation of all moral right? If England sanctions this, what could she answer should Malta seek union with Italy, the Ionian islands with Greece, and Ireland claim independence? And what shall we say of India? Have we half the title to these possessions that the Holy See has to the States of the Church?

The Pope's temporal sovereignty eminently represents the force of moral right, it is a standing witness to the sacredness of constituted authority. It is not maintained by the strength of his armies or the wealth of his treasury. His kingdom is not of this world. And the means by which it is kept independent of this world, are not worldly means. It rests on a title of right, unequalled throughout the universe ; in right it is strong, in human might it is powerless. If you suffer that right to be impaired, you undermine the foundation of all lawful rule, by conceding to man's will the power to subvert that rule whenever it suits his fancy. No human government is perfect, in every country may be found some class of persons who have just ground for complaint ; once admit the principle that this entitles them to stir up rebellion, and you overthrow the strongest safeguard of authority, of order, and of personal liberty. For if you allow man's will the license it desires, how can you secure liberty for the weak?

---

* Romans xiii. 1, 2.

Every true friend to the sacred cause of real liberty is
bound to do his utmost to oppose the organized resistance
to authority we now see in Italy, a resistance whose calm
determined character renders it more truly diabolical,
(though with less outward show of the horrors its surface
conceals,) than even the wild excesses of an infuriated
mob.

Respect for constituted authority is the groundwork of
freedom. What is it that makes England the very pattern of true liberty? What is it which enables us pre-
eminently to designate as 'par excellence' the " gloriously
free?"

> " This royal throne of kings, this sceptred isle,
> This earth of majesty, this seat of Mars,
> This happy breed of men, this little world,
> This precious stone set in the silver sea,
> This blessed plot, this earth, this realm, this England,
> This land of such dear souls, this dear, dear land,
> Dear for her reputation through the world."

What, I ask, is it which enables us to say of this our
England, that, search the world over, you will never find
a country where man enjoys more perfect and full liberty
of speech and of action? The cause of it is twofold.
Englishmen not only ask liberty for themselves, they
respect the liberty of their fellow countrymen. This is
one cause, and the other is closely allied to it. In the
English breast is implanted deep, respect for law, respect
for established rights, respect for constituted authority.
We know the distress which sometimes falls on whole
masses of our population, yet how seldom are riots the
consequence? We know how often some political change
is demanded, yet how rarely are unlawful means for obtaining it had recourse to? however eagerly, however
justly any class of men may desire reform in any particular, they would instantly defeat their purpose and draw
the reprobation of the whole community upon themselves,
if they sought to obtain their object by violent, rebellious,
or unconstitutional measures.

Once destroy the principle of respect for law and for
constituted authority and rights; and sooner or later the
result will be anarchy, and ultimately, tyranny and des-
potism on the part of the many or the few, in the place of
social order and personal liberty.

more than you can injure the soul by maiming the body; but, by that or other means, you may impair the soul's full power of external action, and though the spiritual power of the Popes can never *entirely* lose its external means of action, (for that would be tantamount to its destruction,) still its freedom of action might be so impaired as to deprive us of the *full* benefit we should otherwise derive from its blessed influences, and which, indeed, is vouchsafed to us at present. The world cannot pluck the sun from the heavens, but it can obscure it by its mists; it can never overthrow the Papacy, but it might succeed in interposing its vile fogs and murky clouds between our longing eyes and that sun of God's Church below! We might still see our way, but could no longer bask in the full warmth of those cheering beams.

The temporal Sovereignty of the Popes is the human and natural means appointed by Providence for a divine and supernatural end. God, of course, might have chosen other means, but it is a fact that He has chosen this. He might dispense with human means altogether, but man must never abandon them, excepting at God's command. It is God's way to work through certain means; to expect Him to change His way, and to work by a constant miracle, is presumptuously to tempt Him; it is to throw oneself from a pinnacle of the temple as Satan wished our Lord to do, because God had promised that His angels should take charge of Him.

Now, viewed in this light, reflect how important, and, in a human sense, necessary, the temporal independence of the Holy See is, both to the actual free exercise of the supreme Pastoral office, and to our own participation in the fulness of those blessings of which God has made His chief Pastor the channel.

It is necessary that the Pope should be a perfectly free agent, and it is necessary that all the world should know him to be so. If he is not so he cannot adequately fulfil his duties; and if he is not known to be so the world will not be sufficiently assured that it is really Peter who speaks in him. One of the conditions essential to render the Pope's voice authoritative in matters of faith and morals, is, that he should speak not as a mere individual, but as Pope. Now, perfect freedom of action is universally recognized as a condition that is necessary to enable the Pope to speak to the universal Church, effectually and beneficially, as Pope; and the temporal sovereignty being the divinely appointed means both for securing this freedom of action in itself, and for assuring the Catholic world of its existence, we are, on this account alone, most deeply concerned in upholding it.

But this is not all; besides faith and morals, besides that range of questions appertaining to faith and morals, in which we believe the Church possesses the divine promise of never failing protection from error; there are the administrative rights and duties of her chief Pastor. It is the concern of the whole Church, and the concern of each one of her children, that the Sovereign Pontiff should exercise these powers with all possible freedom of action. The more unrestrained their exercise is, the wider will be the influence of our holy Religion, the fuller our participation in the benefits of St. Peter's heaven-commissioned rule. But who can calculate the evils which might ensue, even in these matters, from the Head of the Church being subjected to the control of any temporal power? Witness the unhappy concessions wrested by Napoleon I., at Fontainebleau, from his captive, Pius VII., but no sooner wrested by the Emperor, than revoked by that noble-hearted Pontiff.

Consider the multiplicity of subjects nearly affecting the interests of the Church, which come before the Supreme Pontiff and the different courts or congregations over which he presides. Excellent as the members of those congregations may be, can we reasonably expect every one of them to be a hero in virtue, and proof against all the influences which might be brought to bear upon him by a secular government, desirous to influence his voice? Even suppose every one of these numerous individuals to be a very angel of fortitude and constancy, it is manifest that prudence itself might often, under such circumstances, require the abandonment of some design from which the Church at large, or that of a particular province, would have reaped incalculable benefit.

Take the case of the establishment of the English Hierarchy. Let any one reflect upon the blessings it has brought with it,—our peaceful synods, the restoration of diocesan action, and the promise of many more benefits to come. But what an outcry on the part of the English Government against it at the first! and what frenzy seized on the English people, or a large portion of them! Not

master in my dominions by means of the Pope's dependance upon him, and, on many occasions which it is
easy to foresee, he would be more of a master than myself.
It is not as a Catholic, I add, it is in behalf of my
Sovereign that I wish the Pope to be independent, and
not the guest of another man......

"I said this, one day, to Napoleon, when the Pope was
at Savona, a prisoner in the hands of France. Napoleon
had a certain affection for me, and knew that the Pope
honoured me with some degree of confidence; he called
me one day, and said, 'Do me a service. I am tired of
the captivity of the Pope. It is a state of things from
which no good can result, and which it is important
should not be prolonged. I am desirous you should go to
Savona. The Pope entertains friendly feelings towards
you, you will speak to him in my behalf, as a mutual
friend, and you will induce him to agree to a plan, which
I have conceived, to terminate this unhappy affair'.......

"I asked for his plan. 'It is this,' said Napoleon, without emotion, 'the future seat of the Church shall no longer
be at Rome, but at Paris'......

"I could not restrain a movement of surprise, and a
smile of incredulity.

"'Yes,' replied the formidable man, 'I will make the
Pope come to Paris, and I will establish there the seat of the
Church; but I wish the Sovereign Pontiff to be independent; I will give him a fitting establishment close by the
capital, I will give him a château, and, in order that he
may be independent in it, I will command that the territory shall be held neutral for a circuit of some leagues.
He shall have there his college of cardinals, his diplomatic
circle, his congregations, his court, and in order that he
may want for nothing, I will endow him with an annual
revenue of six millions. Do you think he will refuse
that?

"'He will,' I replied; 'and all Europe will support him
in his refusal. The Pope will consider, not unreasonably,
that he will be as much a prisoner in your six millions as
in Savona.'

"Napoleon loudly exclaimed against it, strongly maintained his view, alleged a thousand overwhelming reasons. At last I said to him: 'Your Majesty leads me to
betray a secret. The Emperor of Austria has had the
same idea as yourself. He perceives it is not your plea-

sure to send back the Pope to Rome, he is desirous the Pope should no longer remain in prison, and he also has the idea of affording him an existence. Your Majesty knows the royal château of Schœnbrunn, the Emperor will bestow it on the Pope with a territory of ten or fifteen leagues, entirely neutral; he will add, as an endowment, a revenue of twelve millions. If the Pope accepts that arrangement, will you consent to it?'

"He perfectly understood the point of my reply; but he was the strongest, and he would have the opinion of Pius VII. upon his plan. The Sovereign Pontiff answered, as I had easily foreseen he would do, ' That Savona seemed to him as good a prison as Paris, that there, as elsewhere, he was at the centre of the Church; that his conscience was his free territory, that six millions a year were not necessary for his requirements, and that twenty sous a day was enough for him, which he would willingly receive as alms from Christendom."

To rule Europe through the Pope was one of Napoleon's favourite schemes. He once remarked, "Do not fear my depriving the Pope of power, he can never be too powerful for my purpose." What that purpose was we learn from Las Cases,* according to whom, Napoleon said:

"By keeping the Pope at Paris, and annexing the Roman States to my dominions, I had obtained *the important object of separating his temporal from his spiritual authority*; and, having done so, I would have elevated him beyond measure; I would have surrounded him with pomp and homages; I would have caused him no longer to regret his temporal authority; I would have rendered him an idol; *he should have had his residence near my person.* Paris would have become the capital of the Christian world; *I would have directed the religious world as well as the political.* It was an additional means of uniting all the parts of the empire, and keeping in peace whatever was beyond it. I would have had *my religious sessions* as well as legislative; *my council* would have been the assembly of the representatives of Christianity; *the Popes would have been nothing but its presidents;* I would have opened and closed these assemblies, approved and published their decisions, &c."

---

* Quoted by Alison, Hist. of Europe, ch. lvii.

No comments of mine could strengthen the force of this testimony from politicians such as Napoleon and Metternich; but I may add a few words from a speech delivered by our own Lord Lansdowne, in the House of Lords, on July 21st, 1849.

"The circumstances of the Pope's Sovereignty," said the noble Lord, "have this special peculiarity. While, as a temporal power, he is only a monarch of the fourth or fifth class, at the same time, from his spiritual power, he enjoys a sovereignty unequalled in the whole world. *Every state which has Roman Catholics among its subjects is interested in the condition of the Roman States, and is called upon to be watchful, that the Pope may be free to exercise his authority, without being fettered by any temporal influence of a nature to affect his spiritual power.*"

XV.

Protestant testimony.   On the whole subject, the remarks of a Protestant historian, already quoted, will not be suspected of partiality. In reference to the outrages committed by Napoleon I., in the case of Pope Pius VII., Sir Archibald Alison observes :[*]

"Bossuet has assigned the reason, with his usual elevation of thought, why this spoliation of all the possessions of the Supreme Pontiff, by a secular power, ever must be prejudicial to the best interests of religion. 'God has chosen,' says he, 'that the Church, the common mother of all nations, should be independent of all in its temporal affairs, and that the common centre to which all the faithful should look for the unity of their faith, should be placed in a situation above the partialities which the different interests and jealousies of states might occasion. The Church, independent in its head of all temporal powers, finds itself in a situation to exercise more freely, for the common good and protection of Christian kings, its celestial power of ruling the mind, when it holds in the right hand the balance, even amidst so many empires, often in a state of hostility; it maintains unity in all its parts, sometimes by inflexible decrees, sometimes by sage concessions.'" Alison then proceeds in his own words.

---

[*] History of Europe, ch. lvii.

" The principle which calls for the independence of the Head of the Church from all temporal sovereignties, is the same which requires the emancipation of its subordinate ministers from the contributions of their flocks. Human nature in every rank is the same; the thraldom of vice and passion is felt alike in the cottage as on the throne; the subjection of the Supreme Pontiff to the direct control of France or Austria," (and the same remark of course would apply to any control whatever,) " is as fatal to his character and respectability, as the control of the rural congregations is to the utility of the village pastor. Admitting that the court of Rome has not always shown itself free from tramontane influence, it has at least been less swayed than if it had had its residence at Vienna or Paris; supposing that the conclave of the Cardinals has often been swayed by selfish or ambitious views, it has been much less exposed to their effects than if it had been wholly dependent on external potentates for support. Equity in judgment, whether in temporal or spiritual matters, can never be attained but by those who are independent of those to whom the judgment is to be applied; coercion of vice, whether in exalted or humble stations, can never be effected by those who depend upon that vice for their support; the due direction of thought can never be given but by those who are not constrained to bend to the thoughts of others. *It will ever be the great object of tyranny, whether regal or democratic, to beat down this central independent authority; to render the censors of morals subservient to the dominant power; and, under the specious pretence of emancipating mankind from spiritual shackles, in effect to subject them to a far more grievous temporal oppression.*"

I am tempted to add the following extract from another historian, at the time a Swiss Protestant minister, though now, by God's grace, a Catholic. In his celebrated life of Innocent III., Hurter thus writes:—

" If Christianity has not been trampled down as a sect in a corner of the globe; if it has not been reduced to a simple formula, like to the religion of the Hindoos, or if it has not lost its European energy in the midst of the voluptuousness of the East, it is owing to the vigilance and the severity of the Roman Pontiffs, to their constant care to maintain unity in the bosom of the Church.''

I maintain, then, that all Christians are most closely interested in the temporal rights of the Holy See, and that it is the duty of all to support those rights by every means in their power. And inasmuch as Christians hold their religion in solemn trust for every human being, the whole world (though the heathen knows it not) is deeply interested in the spread and furtherance of Christianity: it is interested also in the well-being of society, and in the soundness of the political principles which govern it.

Therefore I maintain that the *Religious, Social,* and *Political interests of the whole world,* demand that no sacrilegious hand be permitted to derogate, in the slightest tittle, the smallest iota, from the Temporal Rights conferred by Almighty God upon the Holy and Apostolic See of Rome.

XVI.

Conclusion.   If all this be true, and who can gainsay it? why should I add another word as to the conclusions to be drawn from these truths? Who is there that realizes them, and that has a heart to respond to them, who will not feel bound before God, to exert himself to the utmost, by every legitimate means, to defend those sacred rights? It is no idle contest, it is truly *pro aris et focis,* for our altars and our hearths!—for ourselves, and for our children, and for the generations which are to come after. If we are wanting in our duty now, what reproaches may not echo over our graves! and those reproaches would be just. And, we, who are alive to the importance of the high interests at stake, are concerned not only for ourselves, but for those who know them not; we hold our knowledge and our religion in trust for others, and woe be to us if, through our fault, others suffer who have not the same heavenly knowledge as ourselves. How shall we answer it before God, if we fail in this our present duty?

Let it not be replied, " This is the cause of God, and to God we may leave its defence." God's cause it assuredly is, but if God offers man the privilege of upholding His cause, and man turns aside from the offer, and wills not the earthly cost it entails, he may refuse the honour, but he cannot avoid the responsibility of such a refusal. Most assuredly God will find means to maintain the Papacy, whether by temporal sovereignty, or temporal suffering, or as His

Divine wisdom may decree; but, if we refuse to do our part in the work, will God leave us unchastised?

God promised Palestine to the Jews, and His promise did not fail, but, because they would not hear His voice, a whole generation passed away before that promised land was gained; nor did God exempt those who entered it from hard toil and painful conflict with the enemy. God's promises never absolve man from his duties.

See what God has given us! A Pope, an Episcopate, a Priesthood, which, for holiness, zeal, and learning, perhaps no Christian age has ever seen surpassed; and if, in return, we stand idly by and see God's Vicar on earth robbed of his temporal dignity; robbed of the means given him to fulfil, with freedom, the duties of his supreme office; if we stir no finger to help him in this his hour of need; can we really believe there is a God in heaven, and not tremble at the thought, how, in just retribution, there may fall upon us that severest of all His judgments, a lukewarm, or even a corrupt Episcopate and Clergy. Or He may punish us by the very consequences of our neglect. We well know how the Church in Austria suffered before the late Concordat, through the obstacles interposed by the State to her free intercourse with Rome; we know how every Church must suffer, when she drinks not of the fulness of the streams which God dispenses by the hand of Peter. If we suffer any secular power to impair the pure and full gushing of those refreshing waters at their very source, to tamper with them at the very fountainhead, the drought and the parching which came upon that Austrian Church,* may be extended over all the world! God avert such a chastisement!

Ah! with all my heart I own that we are bound to battle to the death for our orphans and our prisoners; for all whose faith is in danger because their poverty exposes them to the ravages of the spoiler. Yes! their cause too, is the cause of God Himself. But, I say also, that their cause

---

* M. Ch. Lenormant, in the Correspondant of April, 1858, remarks:—"The conclusion of the Concordat with Austria, has terminated a state of things the most serious in which a Church was ever placed, without reaching altogether the consummation of schism. The Catholic element was undergoing a process of slow dissolution in the Austrian monarchy; the Concordat restores to it vigour and life, by re-establishing its independence."

is included in the other, the cause of Peter is the cause of
the orphan and the widow, of the fatherless and the poor;
you cannot attack one without attacking the other.   For
the orphan's sake, let us not desert Peter!   Can we do
so, and not tremble lest God should desert us?

As Englishmen, we enjoy great privileges, and every
privilege brings with it a corresponding responsibility.
As Englishmen, we have constitutional means of making
our voice heard, and our influence felt.   This entails upon
us the duty of using these means; it renders us, each in
his degree, responsible for the acts of our rulers, if we
neglect to do so.   We are bound before God and before
man to speak, to make our influence felt by the statesmen
who wield England's power.   It is idle for Catholics to
complain of the foreign policy of our Government if they
move not a finger to alter it.   If, as Englishmen, we fail to do
our part; if we omit any lawful means which God has given
us, to raise our voice and exert our influence in defence of
Himself and of St. Peter, in the person of our Holy Father
Pius IX., if, even without protest, without effort, we see
Christ dishonoured in His Vicar, and never use our English rights in his behalf, may we not justly fear that God
may suffer us again to lose those rights, which, by His
mercy, Catholics now enjoy as well as others?

Let us tremble at this, rather than at the fear of human
opposition!   If God and Peter are with us, who can do us
harm?—if they are against us, what human protection can
avail?   If it be true that a withering blight falls on the
hand raised against Peter, it is also true that a never
failing blessing accompanies those who fight for Peter.

But, after all, in spite of Lord Shaftesbury and Mr.
Dickens, of Punch and of the Times, I do not believe
that Protestant Englishmen really care much about the
matter; if we shew timidity, we shall only be despised,
and no one will think our cause worth a jot; if we act
boldly, we shall command respect, and may win many to
our side; for I maintain again and again, that our cause is
the cause of England and of freedom, of civilization and
of God.

Catholics require to be known; like the Popes, all
we want is, that the truth should be known concerning
us.   Then let us not fear to show ourselves.   And let no
man say, what can I do?   I will wait for my betters; if
so, we shall all stand waiting for the other, and nothing

will be done.   Oh, my God, put into the hearts of each, high and low, rich and poor, to do *each one what he can, and all he can,* let each strive to influence his neighbour ; let us not fail to use *all and every constitutional means, which Englishmen so well know how to use when they are in earnest.* And let all be done without a word, and without a deed, which can give just cause for offence.   Let us act as men who are fighting for God, as men who have to answer to God for every act, *and for every omission;* when we have honestly used every lawful means which God puts in our power ; when we have *really* done all we can, and done it heartily ; then, but not till then, can we lay our hands upon our hearts, and say, " We have delivered our souls, we have done our utmost.   And now, O God, do Thou the rest !"

In the words of St. Ignatius of Loyola, " Let us pray as if all depended upon God, but act as if all depended on ourselves."   Let us act fearlessly and manfully, with never failing trust in the Heaven which is looking down upon us.   Timidity never stayed the course of any enemy of God or man, much less will it do so now, when the marauder is at the very gates.

It is a noble cause ; a cause worth dying for ; that cause of the Papacy !

The Papacy is the soul of the world.   It is the Papacy which preserves it from moral decay and death.

Remove the Papacy, in imagination, from the history of Europe, and what is left ? take the Popes away, and what is the evident result ?   Chaos, anarchy, corruption ! the will of the strongest, man's only law.

The Papacy is the very key-stone of Christian society ; it is the salt of the earth ; the city on a hill ; the candle upon a candlestick, shining before the whole world !

Its beginning and its end, its only aim, its life, its one glorious object, is, in very truth, the continuation of the Angel's song which resounded o'er the hills and plains of Palestine, on that blessed night, whose return we are preparing to commemorate,—

" Glory to God in the highest, and on earth peace to men of good will."

Sub tuum præsidium,

Regina sine labe originali concepta !

APPENDIX.

1.

I add a few extracts from early numbers of the Civiltà Cattolica; both on account of their own interest, and also because they furnish an Apology towards any person who may think that I have overstated the necessity of the Temporal Sovereignty of the Holy See. It will be remembered that the Civiltà Cattolica is a periodical published under the Roman censorship, conducted by Reverend Fathers of the Society of Jesus, and, if report speaks true, commenced under very high auspices. These circumstances necessarily give a weight to sentiments expressed by it, very much above that which ordinary publications possess.

I commence by extracting the following passages from an Article on " The Civil Principality of the Popes," in Number XII., for the third Saturday of September, 1850:—

" In order that the Roman Pontiff should exercise his twofold office of Teacher and supreme Administrator of Christianity, it is absolutely necessary that he should not in any manner be subjected to the human reason of any other power which might govern his mind; or to any other power whatsoever which might fetter his action. It is needful then that he should be independent, and therefore temporal Sovereign in the territory where he resides. He, the Father, the Pastor, the Oracle, the Judge, the Defender of all, cannot be the subject of any. Then he must be Sovereign; because there is no intermediate station in the social life, between the condition of a subject and that of a Sovereign.........

" Certainly, the Promulgator and supreme Interpreter of the universal law, which is the foundation and basis of every other law, ought not to be, cannot be bound to the law of a particular legislature above him. In the place then of his abode, and that from whence he raises his voice to teach the nations; the pretence of a legislative power, distinct from the Pontiff, is an absurdity. What can be greater inconsistency than to conceive dependant on the law of man, him, whose office it is to set before all men the law of God? dependant on rules by their nature subordinate and variable, him, whose office it is to propose, explain and support that law which corrects, confirms, annuls, explains every other law different from itself?

" The common peacemaker of the peoples, who embraces them all as his children, who leads them all back to mutual love and to respect for the rights of each other, ought to occupy a neutral territory, apart from every contest and every strife, not subject to the military power of any one."

"The spiritual Father not only of individuals, but of nations and of peoples, the director of the consciences, not only of subjects, but also, of Kings and Sovereigns of the earth ; whose oracle is consulted in order to dispel the clouds from every mind, to remove every error, to settle mutual quarrels; whose office it is to exhort, reprove, strengthen in good every one of the faithful, without regard to territorial divisions; ought to be notoriously distinct and separate from the peculiar interests of any one, and therefore he cannot be subjected to any human jurisdiction whatever."

"He who is appointed by God to judge peoples and kings, individuals and nations, in whose person there resides a power of a superior and divine order, cannot occupy a place lower than that of any earthly dignitary. As regards the inferior human order of things, he must be on a par with the powers of this world, in order that, by virtue of the spiritual authority with 'which he is also entrusted, he may fittingly rule the same without hindrance or opposition."

"Centre and Principle of the universal unity which draws and binds together the various and divergent elements that compose the subject and the matter by which he is to act; it is needful that he should be distinct from these same elements, and not subjected to the peculiar tendency of any of them; so that he may imprint on all a common form, and direct all in a common interest."

"Lastly, the first Mover of the whole action of the Ecclesiastical Hierarchy; who directs, regulates, protects by his responsibility, all the inferior organs, must operate in an atmosphere altogether free from the impulse of every other power, which could impede or limit his action. Then he must not, he cannot in any manner admit, in the place where he dwells and acts, another power which is not dependant on himself, and which could exercise influence over him and over the immediate organs of his action. He must, then, be a temporal sovereign, and the extent of territory over which he rules, should be such, that while on the one hand, it does not exite jealousy in other Powers; on the other, it may afford him sufficient defence against the assaults and violence of neighbouring peoples on every side.........

"Because the kingdom of Christ is not of this world, it is necessary (*forza è*) that his Vicar should possess a kingdom in this world.".......

"The soul, who knows it not? comes from heaven, being the immediate creation of God; but from earth arises and on earth labours, by means of the soul, that organization which is intended to serve her as a ready instrument in order that she may operate freely here below."

"Yes, we must come at last to the conclusion that this is the intimate reason, this the sacred origin of the temporal sovereignty of the Popes: the spiritual power itself with which they are invested."

5

" It did not, it is true, manifest itself from the beginning, because it is not a divine institution, but the consequence of a divine institution. It appears later, because the effect comes after the cause ; it required the assistance of various determinating influences to aid it tranquilly to come into action, because the material for its action had first to be prepared by the removal of interposing impediments; but the secret root from which it sprang, the primary exigency which called it into existence, can be found only in the spiritual power which is embodied in the Head of the Church. The independence of this power from every other authority of an earthly nature, the security of this independence in the different functions in which it has to develop itself, the notoriety with which this security must be made visible in the eyes of the peoples, the preservation, in short, and the manifestation of the divine origin of the kingdom of Christ, in other words, of the Church, of necessity require (*di necessità richiedono*) the civil Principality of the supreme Pastor who is charged with its rule. This is so certain, that if the Pontiff were violently despoiled of the sovereignty he actually possesses, but a short time would elapse before he would obtain another. Whatever Catholic people or Prince should receive him into his State, would be insensibly drawn by the secret force of Religion to yield him a portion of it; and so to create for him an independent sphere of action."

" This also furnishes the explanation of that wonderful phenomenon of the constant duration of this civil sovereignty of the Popes through so long a period of centuries, in spite of such obstinate and indomitable enemies. All the kingdoms which have their origin only from earth, expire one after the other ; all thrones which have no other support, no other foundation than this world, have been successively overthrown, whether by the attack of an external power, or through the internal weakness which was the effect of old age. The Pontifical throne alone has escaped this common law, has endured amidst the downfall, which surrounded it, of the others, has ever enjoyed a continuation of life and of youth ; assaulted and attacked on a thousand sides, it has never ceased, or if it has ceased for an instant, it has immediately returned in greater stability and firmness........"

" We have two modes of ascertaining the natural and peculiar consequences of an institution. These are, either the idea which expresses its essence and reveals to us what it requires for its proper life and action; or the contemplation of that which it goes on constantly, uniformly, perpetually appropriating to itself, in the course of its free development. Now both one and the other of these modes wonderfully agree in demonstrating the necessity of political independence, and hence of temporal sovereignty, in the supreme depositary of the ecclesiastical power......."

" Taught by the Spirit of God, and so made conscious of the most vital interests of the Church, the Roman Pontiffs have always shown an indomitable constancy in sustaining and defending the civil power of the Holy See. Hence, that great restorer of the spirit and liberty ot the Church, Gregory VII., ceased not to expose himself to fatigues, cares, labours, dangers, and willingly sustained the contest against all the powers of the earth, banded together against God and against God's Anointed, that he might succeed in the great undertaking of regaining, with his own independence, the temporal Sovereignty of the Papal States; at that time entirely usurped by the Emperors and the neighbouring Barons. In the great mind of that exceeding great man, the one was identical with the other; the liberty of the universal Church was judged to be inseparable from the civil Principality of her Supreme Pontiff........."

" Inspired by the idea of this great model, the successors of Hildebrand never afterwards allowed sacrilegious hands to invade the sacred patrimony of the Church of God, and for its noble defence, they spared neither fatigues nor labours. So that the magnanimous Julius II. hesitated not himself to brandish the sword for a cause so holy, and to lead its armies in person.

" Men, blinded by error, or led away by the impious desire of seeing the humiliation of the Church, do not see, or rather pretend they do not see, in this conduct of the Roman Pontiffs, anything else but the effect of the ambition of rule. If their heart were right, and their mind not blinded, they would discover, on the contrary, the fulfilment of a sacred duty; zeal for preserving to the Church the independence which belongs to her; the desire of maintaining her in the noble condition which she must occupy in the world in order to fulfil the destinies to which God has ordained her, and produce for the human race, those fruits of civilization and order which depend on her free action. Nor can you reasonably find fault with the use of force in defence of a right so sacred and so necessary to the preservation of the world. What say I? find fault? It becomes even a strict obligation of duty; because there is a time when the very God of love and of peace, fulminates His curse upon every one who does not oppose force to the assaults of wickedness:—' cursed be he that withholdeth his sword from blood:' 'maledictus qui prohibet gladium suum a sanguine.' " *

The subject is continued in Number XIV., for the third Saturday of November, 1850, from which I extract as follows:—

" The action of the Church, the only and the true guarantee of the liberty of human personality which she redeemed and set free, incarnates and gathers itself together in the Roman Pontiff, as in the head and supreme mover of this great body. A chief, necessary, indispensable condition of this high office, is its total independence from all lay power whatsoever; both, because without such independence the operating principle would not be free and efficacious; and also, because it is evidently repugnant and absurd that it should depend upon another element, of which it ought to be the guide, the control, and the law.

* Jerem. ch. xlviii. 10.

Now this independence of the Pontiff is not validly and notoriously assured, except so far as in the territory in which he resides he is also a temporal prince, not subject to any power, legislative, executive, financial, administrative, military, or of any other kind you can imagine, which, under any name whatsoever, can exercise an influence over him, and oppose an obstacle to his free action. This is confirmed both by reason and history, which is a living exponent of the true signification of an idea, and forms the authoritative voice by which mankind bear testimony to what is ordained on high by the will of the Creator of the Universe."

" The legitimate, irrefutable conclusion from such a reasoning, is this;—the civil sovereignty of the Pontiffs is, above all, required for the guardianship, for the promotion, for the support of the personal dignity of man, which was restored to him by the Gospel; and the aforesaid sovereignty is deeply rooted in the very nature and being of the Papacy, from which it necessarily springs as soon as favourable circumstances allow this power freely to develope itself. So that it is a natural offspring of the spiritual power itself, considered in the condition of its spontaneous and full development, and it cannot, without violence, be separated from it."

The following extracts are from a third article on the same subject, in No. XV. of the Civiltà Cattolica, of the same 1st series :—

" An aversion more or less manifest to the temporal power of the Popes, has been the constant note of all the enemies of the Church, who, one after another, have sprung from Protestantism.[*] It is visible in Jansenism, in the pseudo-politicians, in the deists of the last century; in the demagogues of our own, in all the pupils of the secret societies. By this mark may be known the two parties into which the world is divided : those who love the kingdom of God upon earth, and those who would banish it that they may serve only themselves."

" If the war against God and His Church was commenced by the devil, since the beginning of the world, by inducing man to shake off the yoke of revelation, and to seek the source of all Truth in his own reason; every doctrine which directly or indirectly is opposed to the safety and the efficacy of that revelation, and which seeks to despoil it of its earthly defences, cannot be other than diabolical and infernal. And since we are led to conclude that, to be envious of the civil sovereignty of the Roman Pontificate, is to be envious of the free action of the Church, and hence of the Divine Revelation, (so far as regards its effect of illuminating the blind world and bringing it back to the path of virtue,) we must confess that such hatred can have no

---

[*] Frederick II. of Prussia, wrote to Voltaire, " We will think over the easy conquest of the Papal States to supply the extraordinary expenses, and then the pallium is our own, and the scene is ended. All the powers of Europe being unwilling to recognize a Vicar of Jesus Christ subject to another Sovereign, will create for themselves a Patriarch, each in his own State.... So, by degrees, every one will withdraw from the unity of the Church, and will end by having, in his kingdom, a separate religion, as well as a separate language."..(Corresp. v. xi. p. 99.)

other origin which suits it, but that of the devil himself; and this is indeed confirmed by the haughty spirit with which this hatred is animated—a spirit of vanity and of pride, and hence the legitimate offspring of Satan: ' he is king over all the children of pride.' '*

" In fact, what greater pride than for one who professes himself a Catholic, to contradict all that Catholic wisdom has expressed in the most positive form, and by means of its most authoritative organs, in favour of the temporal dominion of the Holy See? The most venerable Pontiffs of Christendom, in an uninterrupted series of more than twelve centuries, considered the civil sovereignty not only a thing to be lawfully exercised by them, but in the highest degree advantageous; and through the altered conditions of the world, altogether indispensable to the free exercise of the sacerdotal rule. The most sacred councils have fulminated anathemas against any one who should attempt to invade, and to violate the temporal dominions of the Apostolic See, or to spread doctrines contrary to its exercise of that dominion. The entire Episcopal order, the head, that is to say, of the teachers and pastors sent forth by the Holy Spirit to teach and to rule all the flock of God, applauds and sustains the same doctrine, and forbids the opposite error. All the doctors of Christianity, the most eminent theologians, the men most versed in Divinity, the most profound interpreters of the Divine laws, in short, the voices which represent the choicest wisdom of the faithful, wonderfully accord in propagating the same truth......."

" Whoever has at heart the safety of the religion of Christ, the glory of the kingdom of God, the liberty of the sacerdotal ministry, cannot do less than burn ardently with zeal for the independence of the Sovereign Pontiff, and therefore for the civil principality, which is not only a most useful, but even a necessary assistance to procure this independence, if not in itself, at least in what regards its notoriety and efficacy. There is no doubt, therefore, that the civil sovereignty of the Popes is not an *affair of state*, but an *affair of religion*, an affair intimately connected with the interests and the prosperity of the Church; and therefore, an object most worthy to be promoted and defended on the strength of motives sacred and divine.

" It is not that the Pontiffs or any sensible Catholic have confused, or do confuse the spiritual with the temporal, the dogma of the sacerdotal supremacy with the possession of the civil principality of the Apostolic See. It is not that they believe the earthly dominion appertains to the essence of the Church considered in itself, and that the loss of the one, could draw after it the fall of the other......Every Catholic, instructed in his faith, knows very well that the true and ultimate foundation of the Church is Christ Himself; and, visibly, His Vicar on earth, to whom in the person of Peter, He promised infallibility and never-ceasing assistance; that the Church is the eternal

---

* Job. 41. 25.

pillar of truth, against which the gates of hell shall never be able to prevail; that she, strong in the Omnipotent Word of God mystically embodied in her, has a Divine force superior to all the powers of the earth; and that as in the beginning, clothed only with the armour of God, without any human protection, she conquered and overcame the pagan world; so in like manner, even if despoiled and oppressed, she would issue from days so deplorable victorious over the rebel and apostate world.

"Every Catholic knows very well from his faith, that Heaven is distinct from earth; that the eternal goods to which he tends are different from the temporal; that the life and action of the Church proceeds from her internal principle, which is Christ; that, speaking absolutely, she has no need of earthly support to sustain herself."

"Every one knows all this quite well; it is known, it is manifest even to the rude and unlearned among the faithful; the humblest old woman amongst us can give a lecture to others about it, and we have no need that the foolish wisdom of the world should come to remind us of it. But the question is not this. The question is, whether it is lawful for us to tempt God, and to constrain Him always to work miracles? whether supposing that the Church has to do her work among men, she can, according to the ordinary and natural course of things, do it without human means? whether the most powerful of those means, from which all the others derive their freedom and their strength, be the civil independence of the Supreme Pontiff? whether it be filial piety in us, towards this our celestial mother the Church, to wish her despoiled of all splendour and power which depends upon ourselves, only because we know that this will not cause her to perish from the earth?......"

"Christ founded and sustained the Church at her commencement without human protection of any kind; He enabled her to triumph over the most terrible obstacles raised against her by the might of the powerful, the pride of the wise, the prejudices of the ignorant. This was the most sublime miracle which exceeds all others in grandeur and splendour; in itself it includes every thing of extraordinary and magnificent which has been wrought by Omnipotence, and by reason of it, in order to be persuaded that the Church is Divine, it is sufficient only to observe that she exists. Yes, the very existence of the Church, being on this account precisely, a most miraculous fact; an event which both fulfils prophecy and exceeds alike the calculations of man, and the powers of nature; is in itself an argument and an irrefutable testimony of her celestial origin. But this miracle, from the very fact that it is such, is a departure from the ordinary course of things; it is an exception to the usual law. As soon then as that first necessity had ceased, of showing to the blind world the Divinity of the Church, that Divinity having become an incontestable and conspicuous truth for every one who had eyes only to behold the Church, she must for the future enter again into the regular course of every thing human, and avail herself of the natural means established by God, to maintain herself and do her work through them......

"As the soul in the body; although indeed, at first produced by the immediate operation of God ; still, afterwards maintains herself there, develops herself and exercises her powers by the aid of earthly faculties, and by means of the actual material organs which derive their life from her; so, the Church is at first introduced into the world by the sole force of miraculous and divine power ; but afterwards it behoves her, for her own preservation and for the exercise of her proper activity amongst men, to avail herself of the very instruments furnished by that large body in which she dwells. This is the divine ordinance, this the wisdom of sweet Providence, by which God attains His ends with strength, but by spontaneous and natural means. To desire the contrary is a manifest rebellion against His inviolable decrees, it is an assault against the order which He has decreed for the universe."

"True it is that, should human arrogance wax so bold as to deprive the Church of her earthly supports, God by His power would renew His miracles, and, in spite of man, He would maintain His promise of Her eternal preservation. But this would be the work of divine truth and omnipotence, not the docile cooperation of man, nor the sweet course of spontaneous action. It would show that God knows how, at all costs, to attain the fulfilment of His promises, it would not remove from us the crime of felons and sacrilegious. It would be a fresh proof that there is no counsel or power which can prevail against God, but it would not at all lessen the force of our reasoning founded on what is produced by the intrinsic and natural order of things."

"Supposing then that the Church, existing among mankind, must avail herself of human means, who does not perceive that these would be inefficacious, and as it were null, without the independence, and therefore, without the temporal sovereignty of her supreme Head?......"

"In order that the Church, which extends herself through the vast limbs of this immense body of the universe, may by her spiritual influences elevate it to an end above this world, and overcome the opposition which it constantly opposes to her through its carnal tendencies, it is necessary that her highest power; to which obey and by whom are moved, all her other powers, should be independent and free in itself, should be unfettered by any subjection whatever to any conceivable organ or material part of the body which it fills; it must not feel the influence of any power of this world. And as this supreme power, centre and principle and law of all the rest; is for the Church the Supreme Pontifical authority; it becomes necessary that this should be altogether exempt from subjection to, or dependance upon, any earthly ruler whatever, (whether it be the rule of an individual or of a collection of individuals,) it must be altogether absolute and free, dependent on none but itself. Under such circumstances alone will its action be certain to remain free from the control and the direction of others. Now such independence is not possible, if the person who is invested with this authority is not also a temporal prince in the place of his residence.   Hence such a principality is required by the very nature of the spiritual principle, it naturally appertains to the Supreme Pontificate, it is a condition necessary, in the ordinary course of things, to the free and efficacious exercise of the Priesthood, to the fulfilment of the sublime mission given by God to His Church."

" Hence it follows, that this civil principality of the Popes cannot be regarded as a secular (*profano*) but only as a sacred object; it is not a *state matter*, but, in the rigorous sense of the words, a *religious matter*, and the Pontiffs in so regarding it, have not confused (as impious men blasphemously assert) two things distinct in themselves, but have wisely reunited in esteem, two things intimately joined together in themselves, and of which the more noble imparts to the other a reflection of its own nobility and excellence......"

" All is harmonious in the social system, and the integral parts which compose it go hand in hand in their progress and peaceful advance.   The civil sovereignty of the Popes was gradually produced by the operation itself of time, along with all the other new institutions of Christian culture, along with the refinement of manners, with the amelioration and better definition of the relations between the various portions of Society, with the birth of the different political states, and the altered conditions of society rendered it indispensable to the exercise of the Pontifical power, to the peace and tranquillity of Catholic nations."

" But without this, we have seen that it is a natural and necessary consequence of the spiritual power itself, from which it could not be separated without doing that spiritual power an extreme violence, and constraining it to remain in a state contrary to the exigencies of its own nature, a state which, because of its being forced, could not in any way be lasting.   Nor does the absence of all civil power in the Church of the primitive times, avail anything against this incontestable truth.   Because we must not form our judgment of what belongs to the nature of anything whatever, from the time of its commencement and infancy, but from the time when we find it arrived at development and maturity.   What judgment would you form of a beech tree or a pine, if you were to be guided by their early condition while yet they were shoots, or no more than little tender plants?   Yet, all their essence is contained in them from the commencement, nevertheless it has not yet displayed all its properties.   The child is a true man in substance, no less than the adult and the grey-headed; but for all that, he has not yet unfolded or manifested all his powers; nor are the organs, of which he must avail himself for the exercise of his action, yet arrived at the degree of strength and perfection necessary to fulfil their office."

" The Church as regards her essence, was the same from the commencement, complete and entire she came forth from the hands of her Divine Founder.   Dogmas, sacraments, moral law, priesthood, hierarchy, in short all that regards and constitutes her substance, was contained in her from her first commencement, nor could she be wanting in any one of these parts without the loss and destruction of her intrinsic and natural structure. But all that which is accessory, instrumental, development of principles already existing from the first, was necessarily to come after, in proportion as she went on advancing in strength and growth. Do we seek to find, from the very first birth-time of the Church, the system of diocesan metropoles already formed and flourishing? chapters formed from the flower of the clergy, forming the council of individual bishops? seminaries for educating youth in the sacerdotal spirit? aspirants to the sacred ministry? the different congregations of which the Supreme Pontiff makes use as instruments in the administration of the universal Church? the different religious orders, which form as it were, a sacred militia, and in a manner, the permanent armies of this divine society? the venerable consistory of Cardinals, which is as it were, the supreme Senate of the Church, and forms the body of the natural councillors of the chief Hierarch? The constitution and development of these and similar things, went on by degrees, as properties which do not belong to the essence of the Church but emanate from it, and as organs requisite to the full and free exercise of her efficacy. Even the churches in which we assemble do not belong to the intrinsic essence of religion; do you wish then that they should be demolished?"

"Use the same reasoning as regards the temporal power of the Popes. It is not the essence, but it is a production of the essence; it does not form a part of the constituting substance, but it is an accessary necessary to the free and fitting exercise of the Pontifical ministry. It did not appear, nor ought it to have appeared in the infancy of the Church, but it at once began to manifest itself as soon as she commenced to grow and to spread, and it developed itself fully at the time of Charlemagne, when the Church having arrived at a state of maturity was in a condition to bring forth as offspring to the faith, no longer scattered individuals, but entire nations; when, through the division of Europe into different Catholic states, the Church commenced to hail as her children distinct peoples and kingdoms, and to look upon them from her lofty position, removed from all dependence upon them, that she might preserve them free from mutual jealousy, banded in fraternal love, and at the same time guide them by the paths of truth and justice, to the supernatural beatitude of the life to come."

2.

I again call attention to the fact, that our Holy Father himself in his Encyclical Letter to the bishops, dated the 18th of June, 1859, makes use of these words: "While We reprobate and grieve for these acts of rebellion, &c., &c..........and *while We openly declare that the civil power is necessary to this Holy See, in order that it may be able to*

exercise without any impediment its sacred authority for the good of
religion, (dum necessarium esse palam edicimus Sanctæ huic Sedi
civilem principatum, ut in bonum religionis sacram potestatem sine ullo
impedimento exercere possit)......to you, Venerable Brethren, We
have recourse by letter, that We may find some comfort for Our
grief."

I avail myself of the translations of this letter and of the two
recent Allocutions of our Holy Father on the same subject, which
appeared in the *Weekly Register*, and I subjoin these important
documents at full length.

" *Encyclical Letter of Our Most Holy Lord Pius IX. by Divine Provi-*
dence, Pope, to all' the Patriarchs, Primates, Archbishops, Bishops,
and other ordinaries, having grace and communion with the Holy
  See.

" The seditious movement which has lately broken out in Italy,
against the authority of the legitimate Princes, has passed like a flame
of fire from the States adjoining Our Pontifical Dominions, even into
some of Our Provinces. Moved by the sad example of others, and
excited by foreign influence, these provinces have withdrawn from
Our paternal rule, and at the instigation of a few, have even sought to
place themselves under that Italian Government, which during these
last years has shown itself the enemy of the legitimate rights of the
Church and of her Sacred Ministers. While We reprobate and grieve
for these acts of rebellion, by which a part only of the people in those
disturbed provinces so unjustly corresponded to Our fatherly solicitude
and care, and while We openly declare that the civil power is necessary
to this Holy See, in order that without impediment it may exercise its
sacred authority for the good of religion (which civil power the crafty
enemies of the Church of Christ endeavour to tear away;) to you,
Venerable Brethren, We have recourse by letter, that We may find
some comfort for Our grief.

" On this occasion, then, We exhort you, by your well known filial
affection and zeal for the Apostolic See and its liberty, to endeavour to
accomplish, what We read was prescribed by Moses to Aaron the chief
Priest of the Hebrews, (Num. c. xvi.) ' Take the censer, and putting
fire in it from the altar, put incense upon it, and go quickly to the
people to pray for them, for already wrath has gone out from the Lord
and the plague rageth.'. And, in like manner, we exhort you to pray,
as those holy brothers Moses and Aaron prayed, who ' fell upon their
faces,' and said, ' O most Mighty, the God of the spirits of all flesh, for
the sin of a few shall Thy wrath rage against all?'—Num. c. xvi. For
this end, Venerable Brethren, We write unto you these letters, in
which we find no small consolation, for We trust that in all things
you will correspond with Our desires and Our solicitude.

" For the rest, We openly declare, that clothed with strength from
on high, which Almighty God, moved by the prayers of the faithful,

will grant us in our weakness. We are ready to undergo every danger and every bitterness rather than abandon in the least part our Apostolic duty, or permit anything to be done contrary to the sanctity of the oath by which We bound ourselves, when, God so willing, We mounted, although unworthy, this Supreme Chair of the Prince of the Apostles, the rock and defence of the Catholic faith. Praying, therefore, Venerable Brethren, that all joy and prosperity may be granted to you, in the discharge of your pastoral duty, we most lov. ingly bestow upon you and your flock, as the pledge of beatitude in heaven, Our Apostolic Benediction.

"Given in Rome, at St. Peter's, this 18th day of June, in the year of Our Lord, 1859, of our Pontificate the fourteenth."

Allocution of our Most Holy Lord Pius IX. by Divine Providence Pope, delivered in the Secret Consistory, on the 20th Day of June, 1859.

VENERABLE BRETHREN,—To the grievous sorrow, by which in common with all good men, we feel ourselves oppressed at the thought of the war which has broken out between Catholic nations, has now been added another exceeding great sorrow by reason of the sad changes and disturbances, which, by the wicked endeavours and most sacrilegious daring of impious men, have lately taken place in certain provinces of our Pontifical dominions. You will understand, venerable brethren, that we allude with sorrow to that wicked conspiracy and rebellion against our sacred and legitimate civil power, and that of this Holy See, a conspiracy and rebellion which certain abandoned inhabitants of those same provinces have not feared to promote and bring about by means of secret and unlawful assemblies, base compacts made with the inhabitants of neighbouring states, fraudulent and calumnious writings, arms provided and obtained from beyond our states, and by many other deceitful ways.

Nor can we refrain from lamenting that this hateful conspiracy broke out first of all in that our city of Bologna, which adorned with favours by our paternal benevolence and liberality, two years ago when we were dwelling there, did not omit to show forth its veneration to our person, and to this Holy See. It was at Bologna, on the 12th day of this month, that after the Austrian forces had unexpectedly retired, the boldest of the conspirators, without any delay, trampling under foot every divine and human law, and loosing the rein to injustice, feared not to create a tumult, to arm, assemble together, and lead out the Urban Guard and others, to repair to the palace of our Cardinal Legate, and there to remove the Pontifical arms, and to place in their stead the standard of rebellion, to the great indignation and amidst the murmurs of the better citizens, who were not afraid to manifest their reprobation of so great a crime, and their applause of our Pontifical government.

The rebels then announced to our Cardinal Legate that he must leave the city, who, in accordance with the duty imposed on him by his office, did not forget to oppose such wicked attempts, and to uphold and defend our dignity and rights, and those of this Holy See. And to so great a height of wickedness and shamelessness did the rebels come at last, that they did not fear even to change the Government and demand the Dictatorship of the King of Sardinia, and for this purpose to send a deputation to the same King. When, therefore, our Legate could no longer resist such injustice, or be spectator of it, he published both by word of mouth and in writing, a solemn protest against all that had been done by this faction to the injury of our rights, and those of this Holy See, and compelled to leave Bologna, he retired to Ferrara.

The same evil deeds which had been brought about at Bologna, were also to the general sorrow of all the good, committed in the same criminal way at Ravenna, Perugia, and elsewhere, by abandoned men, who trusted that our Pontifical troops, not being in a condition, from the smallness of numbers, to resist their audacity, would be unable to repress their attacks. Hence, we have seen that in these cities the rebels have trampled under foot every divine and human authority, have attacked our supreme civil power, and that of this Holy See, have raised the standards of rebellion, have removed the legitimate Pontifical Government, have invoked the Dictatorship of the King of Sardinia, have induced or compelled our delegates to leave, after publicly protesting, and have committed many other acts of rebellion.

None, however, is ignorant of the end which these enemies of the civil power of the Apostolic See have in view; none is ignorant of what they desire and long for. All, indeed, are aware how, in the singular counsel of Divine Providence, it has happened that, amid the number and variety of temporal princes, the Roman Church also should enjoy temporal dominions subject to no other power; that by this means the Roman Pontiff, Chief Pastor of the whole Church, without being subject to any prince, might be able to exercise with the most perfect liberty throughout the wide world the supreme power and authority given to him by Christ our Lord—of feeding and ruling the whole of the Lord's flock,—and might be able, at the same time, to propagate with greater ease, our Divine Religion day by day, to provide for the various wants of the faithful, to afford help to those who ask for it, and to perform whatever he might judge to be for the greater benefit, according to time and circumstances, of the whole of Christendom. Therefore these dangerous enemies of the temporal dominion of the Roman Church use every effort to attack, weaken, and destroy the civil principality of the same church, and of the Roman Pontiff; a principality acquired by Divine Providence, by the justest and best of titles, confirmed by the continued possession of so many ages, and recognised and defended by the common consent of all nations and princes, even not Catholic, as the sacred and inviolable patrimony of the blessed Peter. They use every effort to weaken and destroy this principality. That when they have despoiled the Roman Church of her patrimony they may be able to humble and lower the dignity and majesty of the Apostolic See, and of the Roman Pontiff; and with greater freedom carry on a most cruel war upon our most holy religion, and, were it ever possible, utterly to destroy it. This has ever been, this is the end for which those wicked men have plotted and taken counsel together; who desire to rend asunder the temporal dominion of the Roman Church, as long and sad experience makes clear and manifest to all.

Wherefore, being bound by the office of our Apostolic Ministry, and by solemn oath to provide with the utmost vigilance for the safety of religion, and to defend the rights and possessions of the Roman Church in all their integrity and inviolability, as well as to uphold and vindicate the liberty of this Holy See—which liberty is manifestly bound up with the usefulness of the whole Catholic Church,—and, therefore, to defend the principality committed by Divine Providence to the Roman Pontiff for the free exercise of their primacy over the whole world, and to transmit it whole and inviolate to our successors; for these reasons we cannot but condemn, reprobate, and forcibly resist the wicked and hateful attempts of these rebellious subjects.

Therefore, after having condemned and reprobated the violent attacks of these rebels in a note of protest, sent by our Cardinal Secretary of State to all the Ambassadors, Ministers, and Chargé's d'Affaires of foreign nations, accredited to us and this Holy See, now, in the midst of this your illustrious assembly, Venerable Brethren, we lift up our voice with the utmost vehemence of our soul, and protest once more against all that the rebels have dared to do in the above mentioned places; and by our supreme authority we condemn, reprobate, annul, and abolish, all and each of the acts in any way committed, whether at Bologna, or Ravenna, or Perugia, or elsewhere, against our sacred and legitimate Government, and the principality of the Holy See; and we declare and decree that such acts are altogether null, unlawful, and sacrilegious. Moreover, we recall to the memory of all the greater excommunication and the other ecclesiastical pains and censures inflicted by the sacred Canons, the Apostolic Constitutions, and the decrees of General Councils, especially that of Trent (sess. 22, cap. 11, de Reform), censures to be incurred without any other declaration by all who in any way dare to attack the temporal power of the Roman Pontiff. And, furthermore, we declare that these censures have been unhappily incurred by all those who, at Bologna, Ravenna, Perugia, and elsewhere, have dared by assistance, counsel, consent, or in any other way whatsoever, to violate, disturb, and usurp the power and jurisdiction of this Holy See, and the patrimony of the blessed Peter.

But while by reason of our office we have been compelled, not without great pain of mind, to declare and promulgate these things, we nevertheless weep over the unhappy blindness of so many of our children, and cease not humbly and earnestly to implore the most clement Father of Mercies to grant by His almighty power, that soon the wished-for day may dawn, on which we may see these Our children repent and return to their duty; and may receive them again with joy to Our fatherly bosom, and may behold troubles removed far away, and order and tranquillity restored in all Our Pontifical States. Supported by this confidence in God, We are also comforted by the hope that the Princes of Europe, as in times past, so also now with one accord, and with common counsel, will lend their assistance in defending and preserving in its integrity this Our temporal principality, and that of this Holy See; seeing that it is greatly to the interest of each one among them, that the Roman Pontiff should enjoy the fullest liberty, in order that He may be able to provide for the tranquillity of conscience of the Catholic inhabitants of these states. And this Our hope is the more confirmed, because the French armies now in Italy, according to that which Our most dear Son in Christ the Emperor of the French, has declared to Us, not only will do nothing contrary to Our temporal power and that of this Holy See, but will even defend and preserve it.

Allocution of our most holy Lord, by Divine Providence Pope, delivered in the Secret Consistory, on the 26th day of September, 1859.

VENERABLE BROTHERS,—With the greatest sorrow of mind, in the Allocution addressed to you on the 20th day of last June, we deplored, Venerable Brothers, all that had been perpetrated by the enemies of this Holy See, whether at Bologna or at Ravenna, or elsewhere, against our civil and legitimate sovereignty and that of this See. Moreover, in the same Allocution, we have declared that all these persons had fallen under the ecclesiastical censures and penalties inflicted by the sacred canons, and we have decreed that all their acts were null and void.

We were also supported by the hope that these rebellious children, moved and persuaded by these words of ours, would be willing to return to their duty; when especially all know what mildness and lenity we have ever used, even from the very beginning of our Supreme Pontificate, and with what alacrity and care we have never ceased, in the midst of the gravest difficulties of the times, to devote all our cares and thoughts to promote the temporal welfare and tranquillity of our people. But such a hope of ours has completely vanished. For these same men, resting chiefly on foreign advice, instigations and assistance of all kinds, and rendered thereby the more audacious, have left nothing unblushingly attempted to disturb all the Emilian provinces subject to our Pontifical jurisdiction, and to withdraw them from our civil sovereignty and that of this Holy See. Thence in these provinces, after raising the standard of rebellion and defection, and removing the

ontifical Government, first Dictators from the Subalpine Kingdom
ere constituted, who afterwards were named extraordinary Commis-
oners, and later were called general Governors; and these, rashly
rrogating to themselves the rights of our Supreme power, removed
rom the direction of public charges those who, on account of their
narked fidelity to their legitimate sovereign, were suspected of not
greeing in any way with their nefarious designs. Men of such a kind
resitated not even to invade also ecclesiastical jurisdiction, by promul-
gating new laws on hospitals, orphanages, and other pious foundations,
places and institutions. Nor did they refrain from ill-treating several
ecclesiastical persons, expelling and even throwing them into prison.
Animated with a most manifest hatred towards this Apostolic See,
they dared on the sixteenth of this month to gather at Bologna an
assembly, called by themselves national, for the people of Emilia, and
to promulgate in it a decree based on false incriminations and pretexts,
in which lyingly asserting the unanimity of the people, they declared
against the rights of the Roman Church, that they no longer wished
to be subject to the Pontifical Government. And on the following
day they declared also, as it has now become the fashion, that
they wished to be annexed to the deminion and rule of the King of
Sardinia.

In the midst of such lamentable attempts the leaders of that faction
cease not to devote all their arts to corrupt the manners of the people,
especially by means of books and journals, published at Bologna, or
elsewhere, in which they promote the license to dare anything, and
assail with insults the Vicar of Christ here on earth, and treat with
ridicule the practices of religion and piety, and scorn at prayers intended to do honour to the Immaculate and most Holy Virgin Mary
Mother of God, and to implore her most powerful patronage. In
theatrical representations the purity of public morals is offended, as
well as modesty and virtue; and persons consecrated to God are exposed to the common contempt and derision of all.

And these things are done by those who affirm that they are Catholics, and that they honour and venerate the supreme spiritual power
and authority of the Roman Pontiff. Every one certainly perceives
how deceitful is such a profession; when they who make it conspire
with all those who are waging the most bitter war against the Roman
Pontiff and the Catholic Church, and who make every effort to tear
out and to extirpate, if that were possible, from every mind, our
divine Religion and its saving doctrine. Wherefore, you especially,
Venerable Brothers, who participate in our labours and troubles,
can easily understand in what grief we are plunged, and with what
mourning and indignation impressed, along with you and all good men.
In the midst of such poignant pain we enjoy the consolation to see
that the people of the provinces of the Æmilia, being in by far the
greatest number grieved at such attempts, and particularly abhorrent
to them, preserve their fidelity to their legitimate sovereign, and ad-
here constantly to the civil dominion of ourself, and of this Holy See,

and that the whole of the clergy of these provinces, who certainly deserve the greatest praise, have had nothing more at heart than to fulfil assiduously the functions of their charge in the midst of such a change and disturbance, and to show openly with what fidelity and observance it follows us and this Holy See, overlooking and despising the most fearful dangers.

As for us, bound as we are by reason of our most serious charge, and by solemn oath, to combat fearlessly for the cause of our most holy religion; to protect strenuously from all violation the rights and possessions of the Roman Church; to defend constantly our civil sovereignty, that of this Holy See, and transmit it in its integrity to our successors, as the patrimony of Blessed Peter; we cannot do otherwise than to raise again our Apostolical voice that the whole of the Catholic world, and in the first place all our Venerable Brothers who have the charge of holy things, and from whom, in the midst of such great anxiety, we have received such remarkable and distinguished proofs of their immoveable fidelity, love, and affection for us, for this Holy See, and the patrimony of Blessed Peter, may know how vehemently we disapprove of what men of that kind have had the audacity to perpetrate in the Æmilian provinces of our Pontifical dominions. Therefore, in presence of your large assembly, we entirely reprobate and declare to be void and null all the aforesaid and all other acts whatever of the rebels against the ecclesiastical power and immunities and against the supreme civil authority, sovereignty, power, and jurisdiction of ourself and of this Holy See, in whatever way such acts are entitled.

No one is ignorant that all those who have, in the said provinces, lent their co-operation, advice, or consent to the said acts, or have favoured them in any other way, have fallen under the ecclesiastical censures and penalties which we have mentioned in our aforesaid Allocution.

For the rest, Venerable Brothers, let us approach with confidence the throne of grace, to obtain consolation and strength by the help of the Divine assistance, in such adverse circumstances. Nor let us desist to pray and beg humbly and strenuously of God, so rich in mercy, with assiduous and fervent prayers, that by His omnipotent power He may bring back to the paths of justice, religion, and salvation all wanderers, some of whom, perhaps miserably deceived, know not what they do.

POSTSCRIPT.

The foregoing address was in type before the appearance of the admirable "declaration of the Catholic Laity," which must be thankfully hailed by all who duly appreciate the vast importance of the subject. It is to be hoped that it will not only be universally signed, but universally *acted upon.* I am sure the eminent persons who drew it up will pardon me if I venture to add, that we are bound not only " to resist and resent in the spirit of the constitution" all conduct, on the part of our statesmen, which is either directly or indirectly hostile to the temporal rights of the Holy See; we are bound further to use all our influence to induce our government to assist in the protection and maintenance of those rights. Let not the idea that this is possible, be abandoned as a mere chimera. After the congress of Vienna, England was favoured with the public thanks of Pope Pius VII. Why should she not even yet merit those of Pope Pius IX.? Let it not be our fault if she does not! We are stronger than we know. We have the strength of unity of principle, and the strength also which is afforded by a high and holy principle of action. These are sources of strength no party in the state possesses. We possess them because we are not a party, but the representatives and the trustees, so to speak, of the truth of God. Let us only exert our English rights in every lawful way, and no man can foresee how much may be accomplished.

Since the Appendix was in type I have received the Number of the " Civiltà Cattolica," for the 3rd instant. It contains allusions and remarks too significant and important to be passed over. I therefore extract the most important, although various additions and emendations

have already caused an unforeseen and undesired delay in
the appearance of this little publication.

This last " Civiltà " speaks as follows :—

" Sovereignty, in its fulness, is the only social condition which secures
and makes manifest the independence of the person invested with it,
and leaves his external action at liberty to follow his internal judgment
and inspirations.   A Pope, who is not a King, or who has at his
side a government, which holds the power in its hands, might be
reduced to silence by nothing more than a prohibition to all the organs
which afford means of publicity against publishing his documents,
in order that they might not be exposed to the outrages of a licentious
press.   Thus, without any declaration of hostility,—nay, even under
the pretence of respect, the universal teacher of the world would be
rendered mute by a single stroke.   And, in such a case, which, indeed,
is the easiest possible to conceive, into what perplexity and consterna-
tion would the consciences of Catholics be thrown!   The mere
suspicion of the preponderating influence of a friendly government, is
sometimes sufficient to disturb men's minds, and to produce a sort of
confused agitation in their hearts.   Now consider what it would be if
this government should have the Pontiff for its subject and its
stipendiary!   A dark cloud of doubt and uncertainty, would extend
itself over all he said, or did not say.   Therefore the temporal Sovereignty of the Supreme Pontiff, is not so much a thing which merely
befits the Catholic Church, and a means of avoiding jealousy among
different powers, as it is a guarantee and a safeguard for liberty of
conscience itself in behalf of the faithful, individually.......

" But more, the temporal Sovereignty of the Popes is not only an
indispensable guarantee of the liberty of conscience of the Catholic
world; but it is the only defence which, at this day, remains to secure
the said liberty, in the present order of the social state.   In other
times, the spiritual authority possessed a thousand barriers against the
invasion and abuse of the lay power.   The canon law universally
recognized as superior to civil law; Bishops endowed with rich patri-
monies, and not seldom possessing also temporal jurisdiction ; the
Catholic principle so pervading the political constitution, that the
Prince could not abandon the faith without, by that very fact, losing
the throne; ecclesiastical censures in vigour, and producing effects
even in the civil order; clerical persons exempted from lay tribunals ;
the vote of the Bishops required for forming the laws; the secular
arm obliged to maintain the sentences of the spiritual authority, and
so on.   But now, the progress of illumination has laid a heavy hand
on all these prerogatives of the Church; and after having deprived her
of taking any part in civil and political matters, has sought everywhere
to render her ministers subject to the lay power, by the abolition of
ecclesiastical immunities, and by the substitution of the stipends of the
State in place of the property which belonged to the clergy.   The

only thing which remains firm, in spite of all, is the temporal Sovereignty of the Popes; and by means of this, the Head at least of all the Ecclesiastical Hierarchy, is notoriously his own master, (*sui juris*,) occupying an independent sphere of action, and at liberty to give free movement to the whole body of the Catholic Church. He alone, amidst the shackles which trammel the other Bishops of the world, and the silence to which they are often constrained, can act with freedom; and, from the summits of the Vatican, sound forth an unfettered language which spreads over the whole earth to admonish and instruct the nations. On the other hand, should this independence also fail, the Catholic Church is deprived of every guarantee, it is abandoned to the mercy and the arrogance of the lay power. . . . .

"Nothing can supply the place of the civil independence of the Supreme Pontiff; because no other guarantee can ever be of equal value to that which secures the free influx of the very principle of life and action, into the whole of the large body of the faithful of Christ. Hence, we observed elsewhere, with good reason, that the entire freedom of action of the Catholic Church, is comprised in the political independence of the Popes."

December 17th, 1859.

THE END.

PRINTED BY RICHARDSON AND SON, DERBY,

BY THE SAME AUTHOR.

ARE CATHOLICS CHRISTIANS?

A few words on the Worship due to the Blessed
Virgin, the Holy Angels, and the Saints. Price
one Penny.

THE ROOT OF THE MATTER.

Part I. Price one Penny.

www.ingramcontent.com/pod-product-compliance
Lightning Source LLC
Chambersburg PA
CBHW030001030726
47499CB00008B/2849